# ALL AT SEA WITH TRUFFLES

# ALL AT SEA WITH TRUFFLES

*The Fat Tabby Cat Goes Cruising*

Sheila Collins

Foreword by Ann Widdecombe

APEX PUBLISHING LTD

First published in 2011 by
Apex Publishing Ltd
PO Box 7086, Clacton on Sea, Essex, CO15 5WN, England
**www.apexpublishing.co.uk**

Copyright © 2011 by Sheila Collins
The author has asserted her moral rights

**British Library Cataloguing-in-Publication Data**
**A catalogue record for this book**
**is available from the British Library**

ISBN HARDBACK:     1-907792-97-X     978-1-907792-97-7

All rights reserved. This book is sold subject to the condition, that no part of this book is to be reproduced, in any shape or form. Or by way of trade, stored in a retrieval system or transmitted in any form or by any means, electronic, mechanical, photocopying, recording, be lent, re-sold, hired out or otherwise circulated in any form of binding or cover other than that in which it is published and without a similar condition, including this condition being imposed on the subsequent purchaser, without prior permission of the copyright holder.

Typeset in 10.5pt Georgia

Cover Design:  Siobhan Smith

Illustrations:  Sheila Collins

Printed and bound in Great Britain by
Biddles Ltd., King's Lynn, Norfolk

# Contents

| | |
|---|---|
| Author's Note | vi |
| Foreword by Ann Widdecombe | vii |
| Let me introduce myself | 1 |
| Pre-cruise preparations | 4 |
| Getting started | 9 |
| Journey to the port | 12 |
| Arrival at the port | 15 |
| Checking in and getting on board | 19 |
| Arriving at our stateroom | 27 |
| Around our stateroom | 30 |
| Lifeboat drill and leaving port | 40 |
| The first evening on board | 48 |
| First day at sea | 59 |
| Second sea day | 82 |
| Going ashore | 97 |
| Another sea day | 117 |
| The next day | 131 |
| Life on board | 142 |
| Our last full day on board the ship | 153 |
| Leaving the ship and going home | 159 |

# Author's Note

People seem to have enjoyed Truffles' catty, and sometimes acerbic, comments published in her 'diaries' giving us her take on a cat's life whilst living in our human world. Cruising being my absolute favourite pastime, I thought I would put her on board a cruise ship to see just what she would make of that particular environment!

Obviously no modern-day cruise ships would ever allow a cat on board, so I have used a bit of 'poetic licence' by allowing Truffles to enter this essentially human domain. Also, the 'cruise ship' on which I have chosen to take Truffles is, in fact, a combination of descriptions of my two favourite cruise ships (cruise aficionados will probably recognise both of them!), as between them they have every kind of facility and amenity on board that would interest Truffles.

# Foreword

Ever since Truffles wandered into my life via an early manuscript I have from time to time thought: "I wonder what that cat is up to? When will we get the next story?" And now here it is and it appears that Truffles and I have been doing much the same thing – enjoying life on the waves. For anybody who loves both the sea and cats this book is a dream.

As usual the younger reader will learn as Truffles experiences everything from lifeboat drill to distinguishing between the various decks to climbing the mast to the noise of the engine. Grown ups will smile over the burial at sea of a sack of potatoes and everyone will enjoy the port adventures.

Next time I go on a cruise it will feel as if something is missing – a quiet, observant bundle of fur! – while those who have never cruised may now be inspired to follow in Truffles' elegant pawsteps.

So, get out your deck chair, pour a drink and let your imagination take you to sea with Truffles.

**Ann Widdecombe**

www.apexpublishing.co.uk

# Let me introduce myself ...

Hello readers! My name is Truffles - though my human carer, Sheila, often calls me by other names! I can't imagine why - and such soppy ones as well: poppet, sweetypie, picklepuss (ugh!) and pussypoo (yuk!) and sometimes she even calls me a little monkey! Now, how on earth can she mistake me for a monkey? Beats me! However, in truth I am a tabby cat of some distinction and definitely NOT a monkey. Although admitting to being of advanced years now, nothing passes me by and my senses are just as sharp as when I was a mere spring kitten. During my time living in your human environment I have learned to understand your language purrfectly, though with a feline larynx I am afraid I cannot make conversation except in my own tongue. Therefore, people tend to think I only know a few words, like my name, Truffles, and phrases such as "come in" or "dinner's ready" or "where are you hiding?" etc. I sometimes think how wonderful it would be if I *could* speak human - my, oh my, what a lot of cats I could set amongst the pigeons from my eavesdropping over the years!

Anyway, here I am, ready to tell you all about my experiences on a cruise that I took recently with Sheila. I know that many, many of you humans just love cruising as she does, so I thought I would personally find out what all the fuss is about. Sheila adores her three big C's - cats, cruising and chocolate! Apart from yours truly, she has been a human carer to several cats over the years, has embarked on 35 cruises and has eaten, no doubt, several tonnes of chocolates. So I thought if I coerced her into taking me on a cruise with her, plus a box of choccies, she would be a really happy bunny. (There again, another funny name to be called! I wonder why you humans say that - happy bunny? I've never seen a happy bunny in my life. The ones I used to see in the fields near where we lived always seemed to be looking anxiously over their shoulders - but that could have been because they had seen me!) Anyway, I digress - which I am very good at doing, as readers of my previous books will know - so let's get started.

Firstly, for those of you who have not read *Truffles' Diaries* and so are not aware of how famous I am in the feline literary world, well there's only one thing to do - go out and buy it or download it onto those little electronic machines you humans set such store by nowadays. I don't know why you all have to have them - we cats have never needed extra equipment, just our sharp brains.

Secondly, please pay attention because I am going to give you a quick history lesson ...

Going back two or three hundred years, nearly all ships had a cat on board - the 'Ship's Cat' - and sailors, being very superstitious as a whole, felt that its feline presence was a good omen. Not only was a feline crew member considered to be lucky, but also the cat worked very hard to keep rats and other vermin away from both the cargo and the crew. Some sailors/fishermen would not venture aboard their vessel if a cat were not in residence to bring them good fortune. So, the ship's cat was a revered creature. Its hard work reaped rewards, from feasting on the 'catch of the day' (fish for the crew, mice and/or rats for the cat!) to being petted and befriended by those on the ship, who would often feel lonely working away from their homes and families for long periods of time. No wonder the cats of old felt superior - they were essential marine accessories!

Cats today still feel that they are necessary, supreme beings in the pet world, and the often seen quotation, "Dogs have masters, cats have servants", is so very true! I most definitely feel superior and my own carer has been long accustomed to carrying out my instructions to the letter in regard to feeding, grooming and the provision of home comforts. She wouldn't have it any other way!

Modern-day cruise ships do not have a lucky cat on board - how times have changed! However, for my forthcoming trip with Sheila on one of the largest cruise liners afloat, they too will be lucky (and honoured) to have me with them for a while.

# Pre-cruise preparations

As Sheila has already told you, cats are definitely not allowed on cruise ships - due to the 'Elf and Safety' regulations so dominant nowadays in all our lives. However, because I am something of a feline celebrity, I had received an invitation and Sheila managed to get special dis... disp... dispens... permission to take me with her on this one trip. How thrilling! She always gets excited before she leaves for a cruise; however, up until now it has been the opposite for me. Usually, while she has been enjoying herself in a life of human luxury, poor Truffles has been incarcerated in the local cats' concentration camp - albeit, I must grudgingly admit - one of the best ones around. Still, it's not the same as being in your own comfy home!

I can never understand why you humans wear so many outer coverings and then complain about all the washing and ironing entailed in order to keep them looking nice. We cats wear all-in-one furry cat suits that only need a good lick once or twice a day to keep them looking glossy and smart. Likewise, Sheila has an awful lot of paw covers. I have none and have no difficulty whatsoever walking, running or climbing anywhere. She has all sorts: lots with high heels (how ridiculous), some all strappy, some flat and others that she wears in winter, which reach halfway up her legs - all so strange to a cat. She also carries around with her lots of small containers with handles, many of which match her paw covers. I think these are called handbags. I have always wondered what she puts in these bags. I would certainly never deign to carry things myself (except perhaps small mice, spiders or birds - as she wouldn't be able to pick up one without screaming). I expect Sheila, in her role of my carer, to perform such tasks.

Before we could go on our cruise, however, we had to do our packing. Sheila always takes several days to do all hers - and I'm not surprised, as she seems to take half the house with her. One container (I believe travelling containers are called suitcases by you humans) is solely for paw covers and her handbags. While she hummed and hawed as she collected all these objects together, I counted no less than sixteen pairs of paw covers in varying styles, three 'daytime' bags and twelve 'evening' bags. Ridiculous!

As for all her outer coverings, her boast is that on a cruise she never wears the same outfit twice. Hence, several days prior to the start of the packing marathon are taken up with her poring over lists of what she has decided to take and what accs... access... accesso... matching things to wear with them. At home she never seems to want to dress up for me, so why is she so keen to dress up on a ship? Perhaps she is hoping that her 'Mr Right' might be on it somewhere? Bearing in mind the size of cruise ships, no doubt if he WAS on board he'd be at one end and she'd be at the other and never the twain would meet, as one of your quaint human sayings goes! Still, I wish her luck in her quest.

Eventually, after hours and hours of selecting her outfits, carefully folding them and inserting them into her suitcases, then adding another load of all those sparkly things she likes wearing around her neck, wrists and on her fingers plus most of the contents of her dressing table and bathroom cabinet, she breathed a sigh of relief and snapped all the cases shut: three big cases plus one smaller one on wheels that she intended to pull along herself, also carrying the biggest of her handbags. What a performance! At least she won't have to carry yours truly - usually if I travel to the cat camp or to the vet I go in my luxury travelling basket, but on this special trip I have succumbed to being held on a collar and lead, as I want to be able to observe all that's going on rather than being stuck in a basket where I can't see anything. I always wear a collar but have never been secured by a lead before, so I am not particularly keen on the idea, but I was told that I couldn't go on the ship unless I was on the wretched thing. Oh well, can't be helped - I will have to give a big Cheshire Cat grin and bear it!

Now it was time for my own packing to be carried out! Unlike Sheila, there were no bags or paw covers to take, but I do have several collars - some for day and some for evening, my brushes and comb, and also my travelling litter tray and sack of cat litter, disposal bags, fluffy bed - plus dinner and water bowls and fourteen days' supply of my favourite meaty food and crunchies ... so I must admit I don't travel light either! It may be, however, that I won't have to eat my own food, as Sheila told me that you can get 24-hour room service on ships and so, if that extends to cats, I intend to order nothing but the best cuts of salmon, trout, chicken and beef! One of the ship's conditions was that I could not go into any place where you humans eat - that Elf had been up to his safety business again! Still, looking at the peculiar kinds of stuff that Sheila and her friends have eaten over the years, I wouldn't fancy it anyway! In my opinion, you simply can't beat a good plain plate of meat in gravy or fish in sauce with an accompanying bowl of healthy water or milk - no piles of washing-up to do and no indigestion afterwards! And no headaches either the morning after an evening of drinking the weird coloured drinks you humans seem to enjoy, which seem to make some of you stupid and giggly and others fighting mad!

Between us, therefore, in total we had all Sheila's luggage, as described above, plus another large holdall for my own necessities, together with my bed and the sack of cat litter. Luckily, we don't have to travel on the bus, as a very nice man called Tony, who takes people to ports and airports, will be driving us to the port, which is called Southampton. I don't think that it is anywhere in Cornwall, where we live, but somewhat further afield. I must admit that I am quite excited about this forthcoming journey, because I have never been away from our home except to the vet in the village or the cat camp. I can't quite imagine - even with my brain - just what this trip will be like, so ... bring it on!

After a sit down and a cup of that hot, frothy brown drink that you humans like, Sheila had one last task to perform before we were ready for our departure the following day - our paperwork! I have my own pet passport and - holy cats' whiskers - what a performance it was to get it! It took several months and several visits to the vet for several jabs, but in the fullness of time it was decided that I am trustworthy (except in the presence of small rodents). So I am now allowed to leave the country and return to it, as the powers that be have determined that I am not likely to become a cat burglar in foreign climes, nor start a war, a riot or civil commotion! Sheila had to get all her own travel documents and our cruise tickets together and that stuff called money (which cats never need, but humans set such a store by), put labels on all the luggage items, lock them and haul them downstairs. She always regrets taking so much stuff when she has to hump the cases around herself - but she will not do the sensible thing and reduce the weight by leaving something behind! Once she manhandles the stuff into the downstairs hall, though, then Tony takes charge of it, and once at the ship the porters deliver it right to the cabin door. Talk about being waited on hand and foot, eh? She must feel that she's being treated just like a cat! Still, it will be back to normal for her when we return - this time waiting hand and foot on ME!

The night before our departure we sat together in the lounge - she was watching that large flat oblong box with moving pictures that she likes to sit in front of in a trance every evening. It seems a totally pointless thing to do to me - you might just as well go to sleep, which is what I generally do, suitably cushioned by her well-upholstered thighs. These thighs are apparently a bone of contention for Sheila - she hates them. I don't know why, as they are very comfortable to relax on. She moans about them being too fat, but as far as I'm concerned the fatter the better - more squashy and comfy for me! I'm not sure that we cats have thighs ourselves; certainly mine would not prove so nice to sit on! Anyway, I'd better not mention these thighs any more or I'll be in trouble with Sheila, dear readers!

In fact, sleep did not come to me that evening, as I was wondering how I would enjoy the trip and what was going to happen. It was all going to be so strange - a completely new experience for me. Sheila, too, did not seem to be putting all her concentration into watching the pictures. Perhaps she, too, was looking forward to the cruise and what might happen over the next two weeks. In the event, we both retired early to bed.

# Getting started

Well, Sheila woke me up at the unearthly hour of 6.00 a.m. I have not been accustomed to getting up at that godforsaken hour for many a year now and, despite the anticipation of the day, I was not best humoured until she had placed my breakfast of soft roes in a cream shrimp sauce in front of me. That was only a breakfast treat reserved for really special occasions, so my spirits immediately lifted and I hoped that this was the way things would continue for our luxury trip! After I had scoffed this delicious breakfast I felt in a really good mood indeed and popped out into the garden for my morning ablutions. The sun had already risen and it looked as if it was going to be a perfect day - no nasty wet dew on the grass to dampen my fur boots and not a cloud to spoil the brightness of the blue sky. Seeing as we were going to have to look our best, I spent more time than usual licking and preening my fur, which I was pretty pleased with when I had finished. I wear a colour coordinated fur catsuit in golds, fawns and various shades of brown, which you humans have been known to admire, commenting that I look like a tabby cat *should* look. Well, of course I do - I AM a tabby cat! What funny things you humans do come out with! Whilst I had been attending to my own appearance, Sheila had also been attending to hers, and when she appeared at the back door to summon me in I looked at her in amazement. Never at that time in the day have I seen her looking so well dressed and smart! Well, I thought as I returned into the house, we do look (as they say in Cornwall) an 'ansome pair! Let's hope that other people think we do, too, and we make an impression when we board this big ship. I was beginning to get really quite excited now ...

Whilst I waited impatiently, Sheila fussed around checking the cooker and cold-making cupboard (a freezer, I think you call it), all the rooms and all the electric switches (those mysterious little square things with which she can make rooms light or black - all totally incomprehensible to me) and making sure that all the doors and window were locked - in case we might get our own cat burglars, perhaps? Then she looked at her watch and announced to me that Tony would be here shortly so she would have to put me on my lead. Well, that took a bit of pleasure out of everything, but I held my tongue, knowing that without the wretched thing I would not be allowed to go on our trip. So I gave her my best Cheshire cat grin - through gritted teeth - and let her clip it onto my collar. I was wearing a new collar - pale cream leather with gold studs, and the lead matched it, so I must admit I did look quite trendy and smart. Well, there we were, all ready for the off, dressed to kill - no, well, perhaps that was rather an unfortunate turn of phrase; there would be no killing on my part, as I don't think I would ever find a mouse on a posh cruise ship, unlike the cats of yore on the old sailing ships.

The doorbell rang. Well, I say 'bell', but in our house it sounds more like a strident call to arms! You get used to it after a while, but it has been known to make visitors jump out of their seats with alarm! Anyway, Sheila opened the door and there was Tony, our driver, smiling broadly and then blanching slightly as he spotted the mound of suitcases and bags and, not least, the sack of cat litter! "My goodness," he said, "lucky I've got the 7-seater with me today!" After a few minutes of Tony heaving the stuff outside the front door and then packing it deftly into his motor machine, Sheila brought me out of the house and locked the door behind her. I must say that at this point I felt a little bit of a wimp, because I had never been out of the front of the house before except inside a basket. So it was all a little alarming and, in fact, though I hated to admit it, I felt more safe and secure on my lead with Sheila at the other end of it! I would never let her know that though - Truffles does NOT admit to being scared of anything! Still, I was pleased she was with me ...

We settled ourselves into the motor machine. It was very large, with big, comfy chairs in it that had straps that went over the humans' shoulders (in case they fell over, I suppose). I sat, held securely, on Sheila's lap. The infamous thighs now didn't seem as large as they do in the evenings - I have an idea that I've heard her saying that her M & S 'magic knickers' help, but I'm not sure exactly just what she means by that as I don't wear any knickers myself!

# Journey to the port

So - off we went! I peered out of the side window and felt slightly dizzy for a moment. I am used to being imprisoned in a basket and not being able to see what is going on outside a motor machine when it is moving. It did seem to be going much faster than I realised, but after a few minutes I became accustomed to it and all was fine. I have never spent much time on a motor machine 'experience', as the vet is only five minutes away and it takes around twenty minutes to get to the cat camp. I have managed to bear those journeys okay, although I hate being in the basket and howl and yowl continually all the way - not because I am unduly frightened, but as it always seems to lead to an unpalatable destination I make my feelings apparent. An unfortunate side effect is that screeching incessantly for that length of time gives me rather a sore throat! Well, there was no need for yowling today, as I was not in the dreaded basket.

Sheila and Tony were talking non-stop like a pair of demented budgerigars on speed, catching up with the events of the past six months since she had last been on a cruise. I listened vaguely, not taking much interest. At this rate, their chattering plus the constant flashing of blurred scenery past my window would lull me to sleep for the few minutes (I thought, in my innocence) left of the journey to Southampton, our destination. However, I suddenly jerked awake. I heard Sheila ask Tony how long the journey would take and he replied, "Four hours". "Four hours??!!" I squeaked. How could I bear to be stuck in the motor machine for FOUR hours?! Oh well, that's going to start things off well, I thought to myself irritably. Suddenly all the joys of the day had gone. However, there was not much I could do about it, so I curled into a ball and switched my main control to sleep mode. Hopefully, the tedious time would pass by and I would wake up refreshed at the side of the giant ship in a much better mood.

Suddenly I was awoken by Sheila shaking me and saying, "Wakey wakey, Truffles," and I realised that the motor machine had stopped. But where was the big ship? I couldn't see anything outside the window except a building that looked like a big house with a sign outside it showing a picture of a human in a cooking outfit and a tall white hat. Tony got out of the motor machine, came around to Sheila's door and opened it. She got out somewhat stiffly and put me on the ground, and my legs felt all wobbly for a moment! However, they soon got back to full strength and I enjoyed a nice relaxing stretch that ran all along my backbone. After that I was fit for anything that came my way! But I was still feeling bewildered. Sheila had told me that the cruise ship would be unlike anything I'd ever seen before and absolutely gigantic - but it certainly wasn't around here anywhere! We walked over to where some tables and chairs were set out in the sunshine. Tony and Sheila were drinking that brown frothy stuff again and had asked for some things called 'toasted tea cakes'. Now how ridiculous is that? Even I know that humans drink tea and eat cakes and you don't toast tea! I know, I know, it all sounds absurd, and indeed it IS to we cats, but you humans just do the funniest things.

While they were eating this strange repast, I lay on the ground and looked at Tony's motor machine more closely. I must say it was very shiny. It was like gazing into a looking glass - and believe me, dear readers, I often look at and admire myself in a looking glass! Mind you, I had noticed that where we had been sitting inside was also totally immaculate, as was Tony himself. Dressed in a smart navy blay... blaeez... blazz... coat and matching tie with badge, he could have chauffeured royalty about. I felt that Sheila was lapping up being treated with such deference and travelling in such luxury! Everywhere else she goes it's on a bus! As I said earlier, make the most of it, dear, because when we're at home it's me who gets treated like royalty. Mind you, on reflection, she deserves to have little treats from time to time - she does look after me very well indeed and most of the time I have no complaints!

After the coffee and mysterious 'tea cakes' had disappeared, so did Sheila for five minutes, leaving me in the hands of Tony. He strolled around with me and gave me a few nice pats. I activated the engine, which sets my purr running. That seemed to please him and we remained companionably together until Sheila reappeared and we all got back into the motor machine. "Halfway there now," said Tony, and off we went in the direction of Southampton. I watched out of the window for a short while, but then curled up again on those thighs (sorry!) and dozed ...

# Arrival at the port

I awakened as we came to a stop. I looked out of the front window and saw a large archway in front of us and a very important-looking human - though with a rather fierce expression on his face - standing guard. Tony opened his window and said that we were catching the ship. "Just a minute, sir," said the fierce personage, "what's THAT?" He pointed at me. I bristled. What did he mean? What's THAT?! I'm not a that, I'm a CAT! "It's a cat," said Tony, rather unnecessarily I thought. Wasn't it obvious that I was a cat? Surely Fierceface couldn't be *that* stupid?! "Well, you can't bring it in here," was the response. I drew myself up like a feline spring and felt Sheila's hold around me tighten. "It's quite okay," she said. "I have a special pass for Truffles here from the cruise company. She is an honoured guest on their ship." She handed over a document to the man, whose face by now was looking rather puffed up and an unbecoming shade of purple. "Well, I've never heard anything like it," he spluttered. "Nothing like this has ever happened here before!" "Well, it has now," retorted Tony smartly, "so, IF you wouldn't mind ...," and he drove on through the archway, leaving the man staring after us in a rather stupefied state! Sheila and Tony burst into that horrible raucous sound you humans call laughter - something that only the hyena members of the worldwide cat family can compete with - and I thought: well, that's one to us, nil to Fierceface!

Yes! I AM a cat!

Still giggling to ourselves, we drove to the dockside and finally arrived next to what I thought was a mountain with windows. THIS was the ship! Well, Sheila had told me, but I just could not believe what was before my eyes. Never in my entire life had I seen anything so BIG! I had heard Sheila telling her non-cruising friends sometimes that they would not believe the size of cruise ships nowadays, so of course to me, being a cat-sized person, it would seem even more enormous. When Tony came around again to open the door for us to get out, I held back a bit - it was really quite intimidating. I felt safer in the motor machine. Sheila, however, realised that it was something of a startling experience for me, so she smoothed me down and whispered to me that everything was fine, she was here, and I would be okay. Lots of people were looking forward to meeting me and I must show them how confident I am - after all, I am quite a well-known celebrity on the feline literary circuit and I mustn't let my public down! Of course, she was right - I was just having a nervous blip. I pulled myself together, put on my arrogant look, and together we stepped down onto the kee... quee... qua... bit of ground by the side of the ship.

Whilst we stood looking at the crowds of other humans that were also milling around, Tony opened up the back of the motor machine and took out our luggage. Seeing him do this, a nice human dressed in smart nautical overalls came up with a big smile and said he would put our cases on board the ship - although when he saw the large amount he paled slightly and said he'd better fetch a larger trolley (yes, I got the word right - trolley, a portable platform on wheels for transporting things!) The nice young man with our luggage then disappeared - never to be seen again, I thought, but Sheila reassured me that it would turn up right outside our cabin, or rather 'stateroom', as cabins are called on the ships Sheila travels on. "Well, I'll be off then," said Tony. "See you here when you get back." We waved goodbye and then walked together to the grand entrance of the embarkation (yes, another big word I have learned!) hall, Sheila trailing her case on wheels behind her and holding my lead and her large handbag in her other paw.

As I was walking I could see that lots of people were just staring and staring at us! Some were smiling, others appeared surprised and a few looked as if they had seen a ghost! Well, I've always enjoyed attention, so I began to revel in it. I was definitely going to enjoy this cruise, no doubt about it!

When we arrived at the entrance there were several very attractive lady humans waiting to receive the oncoming passengers, all dressed in smart nautical apparel (the receptionists, I mean, not the passengers - most of *them* were dressed quite casually for travelling, although there were also quite a lot of smart ones like Sheila). When they saw me, the lead welcome lady reached down and patted me and said, "So this is Truffles, is it? We were expecting her. We're so glad to have her on board." What a nice welcome, I thought. I nuzzled against her navy skirt – perhaps, on second thoughts, not the best thing to do when my fur is gold and brown! However, I am brushed regularly, so I don't think I made her look any the less smart. She pointed in the direction of a long line of desks with humans sitting behind them, and told us to go on over there after Sheila had completed a health declaration form - that Elf was still keeping busy! The shipping line was very particular about trying to keep any infectious form of humans' illnesses from getting on their ships - as indeed they should be! I totally agree and I took on board (excuse the pun!) all their reasons why I should not be allowed in places where human food was served, etc. I, too, am glad that Sheila keeps up with my regular vaccinations, and arranged my additional ones for this cruise, and that I am kept as free from illness as possible. To date I've never had any illnesses in my life, so it must work!

# Checking in and getting on board

We wandered towards the bank of check-in desks and Sheila looked for the one designated for the top tier of past cruisers, as she had travelled many times with this cruise line. There was virtually no queue there, but at the other desks I could see lines and lines of people waiting. I had never seen so many humans in one spot in my entire life - in fact, I had never seen so many humans in my entire life, full stop! I was quite mesmerised by the sight and, judging by the looks I was getting, I was mesmerising some other people as well! I preened myself - my faithful readers know that I always like being the centre of attention!

Sheila was greeted at the desk by another smartly dressed lady, and she passed over our tickets and passports. The desk was high, so I couldn't see over it, but the lady stood up, bent over and greeted me too. How nice and polite of her! She told Sheila that they had never had a cat on board and that I had been quite a talking point in the staffroom! "Oh well," said Sheila, "it's a one-off really. Truffles is going to give us her observations on cruising in her latest book - she is well known for her feline slant on human life and activities. As I love cruising so much, she knows it's an activity of many, many of us, so that is her next project!" "Oh dear, then," was the reply, "we'll all have to mind our P's and Q's, won't we?" Anyway, documents taken care of, Sheila was handed her boarding pass/stateroom key and, after being wished a very happy trip by the check-in lady, we were on our way to the embarkation stage. It all seemed very complicated to me - after all, I bet the cats in olden days just climbed up the mooring ropes and jumped onto the deck with none of the fuss and palaver we were having today.

Next stop was taking our place at the end of a queue of people all waiting to go through an archway, where another official-looking human, smiling and jolly (definitely not so fierce-looking as the one we had met earlier, when we first arrived), was awaiting us, holding a gadget in his hand that occasionally gave out bleeps - or squeaks, rather like a mouse just as it's being grabbed around the neck ... aaah, what a pleasant thought! By the side of this person was a raised moving platform going into a tunnel. It all looked very suspicious to me and I shrank back nearer Sheila - I hoped she wasn't going to put me through the tunnel. In the event, she loaded her case on wheels and her bag onto it, not me as well, and they disappeared from sight into the tunnel.

It was now our time to approach the archway. The man smiled down at me and gave me a pat. "I'd been told to look out for you," he said. "We've never had a cat here before." Yes, yes, I thought - get on with it, change the record! He took hold of my lead and encouraged me to step through the arch. I braced myself getting a grip on the floor with my claws. No way was I venturing through - what would happen to me and what would I find on the other side? "Go on, Truffles," said Sheila, "It's okay - really." I gave her a doubtful look over my shoulder. The people standing behind her were laughing. That got me a bit riled, so I leapt forward, nearly knocking the official over as I did so. This brought forth more laughter. My tail was swishing vigorously; all of a sudden things had changed. I don't like people laughing at me. I tried to pull away from the man, but he hung on to the lead like grim death!

"Better come on through, madam," he said to Sheila. "I don't want to let your cat escape - you might lose it for ever!" Now that riled me even more. I didn't want to feel that I was a prisoner - which is what you are if you have a need to escape! That's what we think of doing from the cat camp perhaps, but NOT from a luxury cruise ship. Also, I do not like being referred to as 'it'. What a cheek! I am Truffles, not 'it'. If he had referred to me as 'her', that would have been marginally better. I scowled at him - he didn't seem so smiley and jolly now.

Sheila came through the arch and - blow me - his little gadget started squeaking! It turned out that she was wearing a large time-telling machine on her wrist and that had set the thing off. I don't know why, but there again I do not in the least understand all the tek... teckn... techno... complicated bits of equipment you all insist on having about your person. I have often wondered why there seem to be so many deaf humans walking about, particularly young ones, with stoppers in their ears connected by wires to small flat boxes. How strange. Perhaps it helps them hear better? Cats, of course, have extremely sharp ears, so we have no need for any hearing aids. Also, talking of small flat boxes, nowadays you also see nearly every human clutching one of these strange objects and sometimes talking at them! I begin to wonder about you all, really I do!

Anyway, I digress ... where was I? Oh yes, we'd just cleared the security archway. On to the next stage ... Would we ever actually get on board this ship? I asked myself!

Sheila retrieved her luggage from the other side of the mysterious tunnel and once more we started walking until we arrived at another set of doors, where there was yet another line of people waiting. What's happening now? I wondered. This 'getting on a ship' business was beginning to feel very complicated and I just hoped it would all be worth it when we eventually made it on board. The people shuffled slowly forward, and when we got to the other side of the doors I could see two more smartly dressed people - good-looking young male humans this time. The sight of these two, I noticed, made Sheila stand more upright and draw in her stomach - maybe the M & S magic knickers were in need of some help! As we approached them I could see that they were holding those peculiar gadgets you humans use that somehow make pictures. These objects I do understand, however, as I have faced many of them in recent years following the publication of my diaries. In fact, I like having my picture taken - it makes me feel important! The young men greeted us cheerily. Yes, the same old chestnut - they were expecting me! At least it did show how well organised this cruise line was - they take several thousand humans on board for each trip, but all the staff seemed clued up that I was arriving! Sheila and I posed in front of a large background with an effigy of the ship. She held me in front of her and I painted on my smiley face. She, too, was doing her best to look attractive - I'm not sure if she was winning! I know that, unlike me, she doesn't like having her picture taken, and since I've been doing my writing she has never had so many pictures taken or appeared in so many newspapers and magazines!

"Right, Truffles," she said, "we're nearly there now! Let's go!" Waving goodbye to the two fo... foto... fotog ... picture takers, we set off again. By now, I was beginning to get a little paw-sore, so I was looking forward to the moment when we could sit down again and I could have a long-overdue nap. I always try to nap for 22 hours out of every 24, but somehow today I felt that wasn't going to happen!

Well, the next obstacle we faced was a rather frightening - to me - kind of staircase, which seemed to be moving. I looked closely at it and, yes, it was definitely moving! How very odd - the one we have at home doesn't move. I began to feel as if I was in some kind of weird dream. In just one morning I had seen so many things that I could never have imagined. Still, I pulled myself together. I had wanted to come on this trip to see why Sheila was so addicted to cruising, so I mustn't be a wimp and let myself be scared merely by the unknown. Cats do not admit to being scared even if they are; it's not in our nature. In any case, if cruising was scary, then nobody would do it. After these sensible thoughts had run through my mind I felt suddenly better. This was an adventure for me and I would treat it as such - and, what's more, I would enjoy it!

So I made a leap towards the moving staircase, only to be jerked back on the lead by Sheila and told that I had to be carried on it! I felt quite humiliated - why couldn't I walk on it like everyone else? Oh well, not to worry - just so long as she doesn't drop me! In a few moments we reached the top of this moving edifice, and I must say that whilst being carried I did have the chance to look around and back down the stairway, and the size of the hall we had come through seemed absolutely enormous. Once more, I had to admit to myself that I was pleased to be attached to Sheila on my lead - I never thought I would say that - as I would have dreaded getting lost around these parts. It was all so very different from Cornwall!

Surely we must be nearly there now, I thought. We appeared to be in a covered pathway and we carried on walking, and walking, and walking. The path seemed to zigzag and we also appeared to be climbing. To me, it just seemed to make the journey longer and, given the option, I would have simply climbed up vertically to reach the eventual space where the path finished!

Sheila slowed her pace, as several fellow travellers had halted in front of us. They were all dragging along their cases on wheels, just like her, only they didn't have any cats accompanying them. Those nearest to us smiled and made flattering comments about me to Sheila. How pleasant, I thought - if everyone we met on the cruise ship was going to be like that, the experience would certainly exceed my expectations! I was definitely on a high right now, that's for sure.

We gradually moved forward and then faced two more smartly dressed, smiling officials, who were manning another curious machine, which interestingly was making regular dinging or pinging noises - not so much like a squeezed mouse, but more the sound of Sheila tapping a spoon against my dinner bowl when I am summoned in for a meal. Again, a pleasing sound to a cat's ear! We stepped up to the machine and Sheila peered into a tiny aperture, whereupon a ping sounded. The official gestured that she should hold me up to the opening as well, so she did so, and I got a ping too. What fun! Now we were only a few steps away from the doorway that allowed us entrance to the ship itself - at last!

We carried on our way, and once on board we were met by a long line of yet more smartly dressed and smiling humans - both men and lady humans this time - and they were holding trays in their paws with lots of those glasses of bubbly liquid that you all love to drink. Sheila was no exception. She took a glass, somehow managing to hold it, plus her bag, her case on wheels and my lead, and we moved on a little to where a group of other newly arrived passengers were sitting chatting and emptying their glasses. We had arrived - our cruise was about to begin!

By the way, Sheila told me later on that, despite my thinking that it seemed as if it had taken half a day to get on board, leaving

Tony's motor machine to receiving the glass of bubbly had actually only taken about fifteen minutes - amazing! This cruise line was just so well organised she said. I suppose it had seemed much longer to me because it was all so new and bewildering and I hadn't known what to expect.

I sat down gratefully whilst Sheila found herself a comfy chair and deposited her case and bag beside her. She soon started talking to the people around her, and as they all seemed to be staring at me I assumed I was the topic of conversation. And quite rightly so - I enjoy being the centre of attention, as you will have gathered by now! I didn't bother to try to eavesdrop, as I was much too interested in looking at what was going on all around me. More and more passengers were arriving and the seating area in the large gathering place of the ship - the centrium, I believe it is called - was filling up. Ship people, smartly dressed in trendy nautical uniforms, were scurrying about refilling their trays with bubbly, and the more the passengers drank it, the more they smiled and laughed - there were obviously going to be a lot of happy bunnies on this cruise! Sheila would be no exception, I was sure of that - after only two glasses of the stuff she was already chattering away avidly with the people next to her, paws waving excitedly and with a big smile on her face.

A little later her new companions said they were going to have something to eat and asked if we would care to join them. However, Sheila looked ruefully down at me and replied that, although she would have loved to go with them, she could not go to the eating area because she couldn't take me in there. Whoops! Oh dear, well, I was sorry about that, but then she had known that would be the case before we came on the ship. Her new-found friends said they understood and they all agreed to meet up later that evening. They patted me on the head, I gave the appropriate polite purr in return, and then off they went.

I felt a bit bad that Sheila was left behind, but surely she wasn't starving after her toasted tea and cake with Tony earlier, and she would only miss out on this one initial meal. Throughout the rest of the cruise she would eat in one or other of the many food places on board and I would dine in solitary splendour in our stateroom. As she usually moans on her return home from a cruise that she has put on so much extra weight, with the prospect of fourteen days of gas... gast... gastro... wonderful food ahead, I don't think she was particularly upset about not eating for just a few hours more!

Up came another smiley, handsome young ship person, offering yet another glass of bubbly to Sheila, but to my astonishment she refused it, saying that it was time for us to go and find our stateroom and get settled in before lifeboat drill. Lifeboat drill? What's that? I wondered. I was having to come to terms with so many new things today, my mind could hardly take it all in! Still, I am always ready for a challenge, and somehow I thought that this cruise was certainly going to be that!

# Arriving at our stateroom

Well, the next challenge faced me sooner than I had expected! Sheila gathered up the bags and said, "Right, Truffles, onwards and upwards." Funny thing to say, I thought, but what she said actually turned out to be quite appropriate. We walked towards a space that had four pairs of shiny, silvery doors on one side facing another four pairs of glass doors on the other. I have never really understood about your stuff called glass - first you see it, then you don't. Although there seems to be nothing there, when you go to walk through it, you can't. It's hard. You can't see it, but you can feel it. If you can't see it, how does it stop you going through it? It's a proper mystery to me, I can tell you. At home I sit indoors on the mat in front of a large bit of it that slides to and fro at the side of our sitting room. It allows the sun to shine its rays through it, so why can't I go through it as well? I give up! But, whatever, it's my favourite spot in the entire house, because the sun makes it lovely and warm. I do enjoy sitting there watching the birds in our garden, but it can be very frustrating when I see one not three metres away from the other side of this in... inv... invis... glass stuff that I cannot get through! Well, I digress again ...

We waited with several other passengers by these strange doors and from time to time they would slide to one side, revealing a small cave. A few people would get in and subsequently disappear. Moments later the doors would open again and the people would get out looking quite different. I began to get a bit nervous - what did it all mean? What if Sheila put me in there and I came out having been turned into a dog or something? What if? What if? Sheila saw that I was bracing myself and digging my claws into the thick carpeting. "No need to be frightened. These things are very useful, Truffles," she said. "They can transport us up and down to different places without our having to walk and get tired. They are called lifts ... No," she corrected herself, "they are called elevators on this ship." Despite her assurances, though, I still felt full of trepidation, as everyone seemed to be transformed magically after entering into these caves.

Moments later, one of the glass pairs of doors slid apart and Sheila marched in, dragging, I don't mind telling you, a reluctant Truffles behind her. I felt a panic attack coming on. "Calm down," said Sheila, and she pressed one of an array of ill... illu... illumi... lit-up buttons on the wall. Immediately, a ghostly female voice from nowhere said, "Doors closing." And they did! I looked around and couldn't see another female human. Where had the voice come from? I was beginning to think I was hallucinating (ha, that got you, didn't it? A big word that I DO know!) I examined myself, but I still looked like Truffles - I didn't look like a dog, thank goodness! I could feel a kind of movement in our cave and as I glanced behind me, away from the doors, my heart leapt into my mouth - we appeared to be perched on air! The entire wall was made of glass and as we travelled upwards I could look down through it, and we seemed to be passing through lots of different layers of rooms. It's very difficult to describe what I saw, readers, so you will have to use your own imaginations! Just a few seconds later, I was startled by the mysterious unseen female human announcing, "Deck ten - doors opening." Suddenly the doors slid open and I jumped out, almost jerking the lead out of Sheila's hand. Thank goodness we had arrived at wherever we were going! I hadn't enjoyed that experience very much. It was all too confusing. "Calm down, Truffles," Sheila said, "we're nearly there now. You've done very well - it's been a long journey for you and very strange, so you've coped admirably. I'm proud of you." And she gave me a lovely pat. Immediately I began to feel better.

More walking, this time along a seemingly never-ending passageway, all beautifully carpeted. My paws sank deeply into it - it felt most relaxing. On either side of this passageway were yet more doors. I was amazed at all the doors I had seen on this ship - hundreds and hundreds of them, if not thousands. What lay behind them? All these staterooms Sheila had told me all about? I wondered which one was ours. Sheila's pace was slowing - it was a very, very long corridor! Eventually we arrived right at the end of it - we could go no further. It opened out onto another row of ten doors spread right across the width of the ship. "We're right at the stern now, Truffles," she said, stopping in front of stateroom number 1204. We had arrived at our destination. Yippee!

She reached into her pocket – I have always thought a pocket would be a useful accessory, but unfortunately my one-piece fur catsuit does not have any. She brought out the little card that she had been handed at the embarkation desk - my, that did seem a long time ago now - and pushed it into the door. There was another pinging noise - ooh, a mouse perhaps? No, just my over-vivid imagination! She pressed a lever on the door and it opened. In we went. The door closed behind us and we both sighed with pleasure. Our cruise was really beginning now!

# Around our stateroom

Sheila unclipped my lead, dropped her bags to the ground and flopped down onto a comfy-looking leather sofa with some squishy cushions. I made a mental note to try them out later! I stood and looked around me. Well, I thought, this is rather like a combination of our sitting room and Sheila's bedroom at home: kind of an 'all-in-one apartment' - how convenient! Apart from the sofa, there was a long, low table with a shiny, silvery bucket on it, holding a large bottle of the bubbly stuff she had been drinking earlier. I hoped she wasn't going to drink all of that now - heaven knows the state she would get into! As I wrote at the beginning of all this, I'm afraid as a cat I strongly disapprove of the way sometimes you humans drink far too many of these sickly-smelling, coloured liquids, which in my opinion are just not healthy! Still, I have to admit that I have never seen Sheila under the weather, so I presume she has the sense not to overindulge. A little of what you fancy does you good is what I say, and I guess she thinks that way too. Next to the bottle were a couple of glass drinking bowls and another much bigger container (dear readers, was I ever going to escape from glass things on this ship?!) containing flowers. Well, that made me feel nice and really at home; we have lots of flowers in our garden. I like flowers - not particularly because of the flowers themselves, but you get butterflies sitting on them in the summer and they are a delight to play with and snack on. There was also a bowl of fruit (those sweet things that are revolting to we cats!) and lying beside it were several of those printed paper sheets you humans like to read, plus some sort of gadget with rows of square buttons on it.

My gaze continued around the room. I could see a very large and comfy-looking bed with compartments on the wall above it and to the sides where, no doubt, Sheila would be stashing away her various paw carriers (sorry - handbags!) and all the other paraphernalia she had brought with her; that is - I had a sudden uneasy thought - if our luggage did indeed ever arrive, particularly my own collars, bed and litter tray, etc. Better not think too much about that last item, I decided, or I might want to use it before it arrived! There was a unit of drawers with some sort of cupboards underneath it, then some more drawers and, next to those, a single drawer that looked, to me, to be suspended in mid-air, a bit like a table with no legs, with a chair set underneath it. I could see what looked like a kettle and drinking bowls - sorry again, I must remember you call them cups or glasses - standing on the top, together with another container of flowers. I peered at them but could see no butterflies - pity. When Sheila opened the single drawer she saw that there was a fur dryer in it. Another mysterious accessory you humans like looking at - called a m... mi... mir... looking glass was above. On the wall above the main block of drawers was a large, flat moving-picture machine like the one we have at home that stupefies Sheila for several hours every night, and there was yet another large double cupboard that went from the floor to the roof on the wall opposite. Just past that was another door that Sheila hadn't opened yet. At the same time as I noticed that door, she DID go and open it and went in! I followed her, curious ...

It was a room rather like the one at home in which she carries out her daily ablutions, and I could see that it had a water bowl against the wall in which she was washing her paws. This bowl was set in a unit of more drawers and cupboards of various sizes, and almost the entire wall was made of that glass you can look into. Fitted above this looking glass was a bank of small lights, and I noticed later in the cruise that even if the main lights in the ablution room were switched off there was always a low glow coming from these lights. Standing by the wash bowl was yet another container of flowers - unfortunately still with no accompanying butterflies - and several small bottles and containers. Set inside this room was another little room where I could see some kind of silver-coloured pipe with a bulbous end hanging down from its roof. A panel with buttons, rather like the one we'd seen in the elevator earlier, sat beside the pipe. I think you call this apparatus a shower. Horrible things - all full of water! Like the water box I could see round the corner. I often wonder why you humans use a water box instead of a litter box. Having a litter box to scratch about in gives most cats an outlet for their natural covering-up instinct. Perhaps humans don't care about covering up their waste - but then I've always been of the opinion that there is no creature as clean as a cat. We wash ourselves countless times each day from top to toe, particularly behind the ears, and the process also helps in awkward moments when perhaps you are deciding on your next move or whatever. There is an old cat saying: when in doubt, lick bottom. But, I'm digressing again! I noticed that on the final wall of this little ablution room were several rails with some lovely thick and fluffy body-drying rags hanging on them. They'd be nice to flex my claws on, I thought (Sheila doesn't let me do that on hers at home) - and I proceeded to do just that! Oh dear - big mistake! "DON'T do that, Truffles," Sheila snapped, flapping her paw at me in a threatening manner. "Okay, okay, keep your fur on," I muttered under my breath and slunk back into the main stateroom.

Anyway, it all certainly seemed like a home from home. Every amenity you could wish for! I decided that we would be very comfortable living here for a while. Suddenly there was a knock at the main door. I dived behind the bed.

It was the porter, who had come to tell us that our luggage had arrived outside. Phew - relief all round! Sheila dragged it into the room. "Now, Truffles," she said, "we'll sort you out first." I nodded - it was good to see that even luxuriating here she still remembered that she is my human carer first of all and, yes, of course her duties to me must come before everything else. That's what it said in her original contract of employment, and over the years I have made sure that she has stuck by my rules!

Sheila picked up my travel bag and shook out my fluffy bed, which she had managed to squash into it - one less thing to carry. "Now, where shall we put this?" she pondered. "Ah yes, here," and she put it down in a corner between her bed and some large patio doors (yes, more glass!) that I hadn't noticed when we'd first come in. Perhaps there was a garden outside like at home and I would be able to do some bird watching. Good! Exotic birds perhaps! I looked through but couldn't see any sign of green. She slid open the door and went out, so I followed and stood in the doorway. I could see a nice table and two low-lying chairs, but there was no grass. There was quite a decent-sized enclosed area of wood decking (appropriate for a ship, I suppose!) with a fairly low, to you humans, but high to me, glass — yes, it had to be glass - wall topped by a wooden rail in front. On either side of this space were high walls of thicker, more cloudy glass, which I assumed was to keep us away from the neighbours in the staterooms on either side. This is similar to how we are partitioned off at home - and very glad I am to have it that way, as next door to us we have two very noisy and annoying little dogs and six cats, all much larger than me, so they can be quite in... int... intimi... scary at times! Well, I thought, it will be nice to sit out here in the fresh air - our own private space.

"Come and look here, Truffles," said Sheila, indicating that I should move forward. "It's the sea. You've never seen the sea!" What's she talking about? I thought. How can you see a see? Even a letter C - how exactly do you see a C in mid-air, as she seemed to be suggesting? Surely you can only see a C written down on paper, or perhaps there's another way of looking at a C? I hesitated. "Come on, don't be silly," she said. So I walked forward until I was right up by the glass wall. OMG - my legs went all wobbly! All I could see was what looked like blue water, but it seemed far, far below us, with just lots and lots of empty sky above. Oh, I felt rather faint. I hate water (except to drink) and to see such a huge amount made me feel quite queasy and, oh dear, I have to admit it again, a bit frightened. Sheila picked me up and held me so that I could see over the glass wall. That made me feel even worse. We were surrounded by this unending sight of water - my worst nightmare! Those seagoing cats of old may have liked being surrounded by miles and miles of water, but I wasn't nearly so keen! I'd known, of course, that cruise ships live on water, but I hadn't realised there would be just so very much of it! I struggled and gave Sheila a sharp scratch, so she swiftly put me down on the decking again, where I felt considerably safer.

I took a few deep breaths to calm down and Sheila sat on one of the chairs, put me on her knee and stroked me. After all her years of experience of caring for me she knows exactly how to settle me down if I've had a shock or upset, so after a few minutes I felt better. I would be okay. There was absolutely no need for me to go near the glass wall anyway, I reasoned. There was plenty of space away from the edge where I could sit and doze in the sun, which is my favourite pastime, as readers of my previous books will know. "We'll put your litter tray out here, your water bowl here," said Sheila, "and I can also store the sack of catlit in the corner where it won't get wet if it should rain. Rain, I thought, well I hope not. We get enough of that in Cornwall - surely it won't rain on a cruise ship!

After a few minutes more, Sheila spending her time gazing out over the glass wall at the C while I tested out the litter tray, we returned inside. I decided to take a nap in my bed and let her unpack and put away all the stuff she had brought. By the looks of it, I thought, that will take several hours, so I will be able to catch up on all my lost sleep. Wrong! I got into my bed, curled around and prepared to go into sleep mode. Sheila smiled and said, "That's good, Truffles, you have a nap and you won't be getting in my way whilst I sort this lot out," gesturing in the direction of the mound of luggage.

She started unlocking the cases and laying out piles of her outer coverings on the sofa. I watched her out of one eye. Sleep wasn't coming. My mind was buzzing with the events of the day. After what seemed an age, but was probably about three-quarters of an hour or so, the outer coverings had disappeared into the tall double cupboard. Yes, I DO know how you humans measure time. We cats are instinctive about time - mostly our tummies tell us. Mealtimes are the most important times in our lives, and so far my tummy clock has never let me down. I am always on parade near my dinner bowl when the golden eating hour comes around. I was missing my lunch crunch snack today, which I usually have at about one-thirty, but I wasn't holding my breath. I thought Sheila had probably forgotten about it.

Normally I would have given her a real piece of my mind or a scratch, but today was all topsy-turvy so I decided I would let her off. I wasn't too bothered - to be honest I wasn't that hungry anyway, what with all the excitement.

Sheila shut her two largest cases again and pushed them underneath her bed out of sight. I could see that there was still the one with all her paw covers and paw - no, hand - bags in and the one on wheels left to deal with. Lucky, I thought, that there wasn't any other human travelling with her - there would be no room whatsoever for all their outer coverings in here as well! She picked up the small black object with buttons on it from the table. I thought she was going to speak into it, but no, she didn't - she pressed one of the buttons and suddenly the moving-picture screen on the wall leapt into life. I couldn't see it very well as it was rather high for me, but I could hear a male human speaking. Sheila switched on the kettle, made herself one of those brown frothy drinks she likes and relaxed on the sofa. I walked over and lay down by her feet. "This is all about lifeboat drill, Truffles," she said. "We'll have to go to that soon before we leave port." I wondered what lifeboat drill meant. I had heard that human dentists had drills, but I didn't realise that ships had them as well. I didn't even know they had teeth! What was a lifeboat? I remember Sheila telling me once that a cruise vessel should never be referred to as a 'boat'; it is a 'ship'. The boats hang on the sides of the ship. Apparently, the passengers want to be on the ship but do not want to have to go on the boats. Very odd. I dare say all would be revealed in due course at the said drill. People do not like dentists' drills, I know, so I supposed they don't like ships' drills either, but Sheila said that they were something that perhaps some people found boring but were, in fact, very important indeed. As far as I could gather from what she was trying to explain, we were going to be told a lot of things that we should do but hoped we would never have to do. What kind of a carry-on is that? I wondered. Learning what we should do, could do or would do, but don't want to do! You humans and your eccentricities never fail to puzzle me. I shook my head to try to clear it ...

There was a knock at the door. I retreated behind the bed again. Sheila opened the door and a smiling, smartly dressed young male human said, "Hello, madam, welcome back. We are very pleased to see you again on board." He was our personal (purrsonal, in my case) stateroom steward. He was very charming and polite and I could see that Sheila was impressed. He came inside, introduced himself as Eduardo and said that he was looking forward to meeting me as, of course, he knew that I was travelling with Sheila. "Come on out, Truffles," said Sheila, "and meet Eduardo." I emerged from my hiding place and strolled up to him. "'Ello, Trufools," he said. "I look forward to looking after you on your cruise. I've never looked after a cat before!" He leant down and patted me on the head, and I gave him a rather come-hither purr - he certainly was very nice looking as human males go. I expect Sheila thought so, too. They spoke together for a few minutes and then Eduardo left, after telling Sheila to ring for him if there was anything we needed. "Well, he seems pleasant," she said. "Now I really must finish putting my things away."

I watched as she sorted out all the paw covers and put them in the bottom of the big double cupboard and then continued to fill up the rest of the drawers with all her other many bits and pieces. She opened one of the cupboards underneath the drawers and inside it I could see several rows of little bottles of coloured drinks. I shivered - a cool blast of air had rushed out of the cupboard. She shut the door. Finally she pulled open the small door next to this cold cupboard, which revealed another heavy-looking inner door with buttons on its front. After pressing some of the buttons a few times, she opened the door and placed inside it some of the sparkly wrist and paw decorations she'd brought with her. "If you had a collar with diamonds on it, Truffles, instead of just diamanté, I'd put that in here for you as well," she laughed as she closed the door. I wasn't really sure what she meant by that. She had a couple of drawers of other similar-looking decorative things you human ladies wear to enhance yourselves, but it seemed they didn't have to be locked up.

Sheila went out onto the decking area (she has since informed me that it is called a balcony) again to look out at the C. I didn't join her. I could hear her chatting to the neighbours. She had placed a cushion on the sofa for me, so I took advantage of it and did manage to have a quick nap. And delightful it was, too!

Well, I only made it to about thirty of my anticipated forty winks, because Sheila was back again. It was apparently time for us to go to the lifeboat drill. She had showed me earlier two peculiar pieces of kit that we would have to wear around our bodies should we ever decide to go into the boats that we didn't want to go into in the first place. Hers was much larger than the one that had been put out for me - apparently, normally the small one would be used for a human infant. I didn't fancy it in the least, but I wasn't too bothered because, hey readers, Truffles never does anything that she doesn't want to, and by the sound of it I certainly wouldn't be wanting to get into one of the dreaded lifeboats!

Sheila clipped my lead on again, turned off the picture machine on the wall, checked that the card that we needed to get back into the stateroom was in her pocket, looked on the back of the door where some kind of notice displayed where we had to assemble for the drill, and off we went!

# Lifeboat drill and leaving port

As we walked back along the passageway outside, there were other humans all going in the same direction, and they greeted us cordially as we joined the throng. When we arrived back at the elevators, however, I didn't have to worry about having to ride in one, as Sheila dragged me down a flight of stairs ... and then another flight, and then another one, and another - they seemed never-ending! This ship didn't just have a lot of doors, it had a lot of stairs, too! I had never seen so many. At home we only have one flight, albeit with a bend in the middle, but there are only fourteen steps in total. I know this because I like sitting halfway up it at certain times of the day, when the sun decides to shine on the seventh step! On the ship, after two flights of these stairs we would arrive at another similar-looking area with elevators on it, where there were lines of staff directing us to continue going down. At last we reached Deck Five and then had to follow the crowd into a large area with many sofas and chairs in it. We had to wait until a nice, smiley human (It seemed to me that everyone working on this ship continually smiled!) took our names and checked them off his list, and then Sheila managed to get herself a seat. I sat on her knee. More smiles and comments came from the people sitting around us. They all seemed amazed to see me there. I basked in their attention. Sheila must have been getting fed up with explaining the same thing over and over again in answer to their questions: that Truffles, her literary cat, was gleaning information in order to write another of her books on a cat's observations of human behaviour, this time holidaying on a cruise ship, which is greatly popular. The consensus of opinion was that they thought it was a good idea, as there didn't seem to be many books around about modern-day cruising.

The seating area was filling up and it seemed to me that I had never seen so many humans all together in one group. And yet I understood from Sheila that only a small section of all the passengers were meeting in this particular spot - all over the ship were equally large groups of people, all eager to hear about these peculiar lifeboat things. It was getting quite overwhelming to a small cat-sized person like me. The noise of all their constant chattering was resounding in my ears - which are much sharper than yours, remember - and so I slipped down behind Sheila's feet and curled up, feeling much safer there.

After a while, there was a hush in the crowd and a loud male human's voice could be heard welcoming everybody before starting to talk about the mysterious lifeboat drill. I only listened to him droning on with half an ear, until suddenly he said something about the ship's 'whistle'. My attention was caught, because birds whistle and so it's a word I know really well. "You might jump in a minute, Truffles," Sheila said, leaning down and grasping me by the collar. I couldn't imagine why she thought I would suddenly start jumping about! However, a moment later, yes I did! An unearthly loud whistle sounded, not once but seven times, followed by a long drawn-out wail that was deafening. I was ready to run, I can tell you! However, she pinned me to the floor so I couldn't move. Fortunately, the awful noise stopped and everybody began chattering again until the voice resumed and a hush descended once more.

In front of us, several ship staff people were pulling on the body kits, which they called lifejackets, like the ones we had found in the stateroom. They were waving their paws about, showing the assembled people the bits and pieces attached to them. Apparently, there was a light that came on if you were in the water and a whistle to blow to gain attention. Neither was of much use to me, because I don't need extra light with my cat's eyes and I certainly could not blow a whistle. Have you ever seen a cat blowing a whistle? It seemed that, if the occasion we didn't want to know about did come about, and consequently we had to jump into the water around the ship, these lifejackets would be very useful. Well, readers, no way was I ever going to jump into any water! A normal cat just does not jump into water; a Turkish Van cat, I believe, is the only one that might. Neither does a cat ever do anything it doesn't want to do, so no way would I be going over the side! I don't think Sheila relished the idea much either. I heard her saying to the people next to her that if she ever had to - as the man's voice had informed them - hold her paws in front of her chest and calmly step forward from a high deck down into the water, it would be a definite no-go! Someone would damn well have to push her! However, as the whole scenario was highly unlikely, neither she nor I was unduly worried. I believe because of the Elf and Safety people, all ship passengers have to be made aware of even the most improbable eventuality.

Oh well, that was the end of the lecture and so everyone started to move. Probably some of those who had never been on a ship before, like me, and were of a slightly nervous disposition (though I am not) were even more so now! I looked around and noticed that the majority were still smiling and chattering, so I took heart and decided that none of it was worth worrying about. Why dwell on something that is never going to happen anyway? However, my tummy was doing the fretting now - it was complaining that it was pretty well empty, so I hoped that Sheila would soon give me something to eat!

We arrived back at the place with the elevators and stairs and it was just heaving with people. There was no way we would ever get into the elevator, so we started up the stairs again. Sheila was walking much more slowly than when we had come down them earlier! I am used to climbing, of course, so I couldn't understand why she was panting and puffing so much. For heaven's sake, dear, I thought, you seriously need some exercise! "Now you know how useful the elevators are," she gasped to me as we reached Deck Ten once more. After catching her breath we then made the long trek along the passageway to our home from home at the end of it!

Once inside, all was calm and peaceful and I sat down and collected my thoughts. However, I then had another rude awakening with a sound I have never ever heard before. Sheila had gone into the ablution room for a few moments and then I heard a tremendous whooshing sound that reminded me of the times she used her water box at home, but the sound here was magnified and speeded up about a hundred times I should think! WHAT on earth was that? I thought. She came out chuckling. "I bet that frightened you," she said. "Yes, it did," I muttered under my breath. "Ships' loos are very powerful," she explained. "Everybody remarks on it. Don't worry, it won't hurt you as long as you don't fall into it. I wouldn't want to think you got yourself flushed down the loo!" She started laughing to herself again. I don't know what she thought was so funny. I'm not a fool - I would most certainly keep my distance!

"We'll be leaving in a few minutes, Truffles," said Sheila. "I'll open my bottle of champers and I think I'll sit on the balcony and have a glass and watch as we leave Southampton." Well, I thought, she's thinking of drinking, so hopefully it will only be a matter of time before she thinks of food, and then perhaps I'll get lucky and she'll give me my dinner. At home I just would not have tolerated her being late with my meal, but with all the goings-on today, I told myself again, I would just have to grin and bear it!

I watched as she picked up the bottle. She was muttering to herself that she had seen other people open bottles like this, so knew how to do it, but hadn't actually opened one herself before. This might be interesting then, I thought. "I'd better put a towel around it," she said, and fetched a small body-drying rag from the ablution room. (So that's what they're called, are they - towels? I must remember that, I told myself. I'm always looking to add to my vocabulary of human words!) She wrapped the towel around the neck of the bottle and prised off a top covering that looked like a miniature birdcage to me. Then she held the bottle at an angle and started to twist something slowly from its neck. Suddenly there was a tremendous bang and the 'something' flew out of the bottle and hit the stateroom door! It sounded like a gunshot! I used to hear these shots sometimes from the fields behind us where we once used to live. All of a sudden Sheila was holding the bottle and trying to pour some of its contents into a glass, but it was fizzing and frothing over - so the towel was coming in very useful! "Goodness," she exclaimed, "the people next door will think I've murdered someone!"

Anyway, she finally succeeded in pouring a glassful of the bubbly from the bottle, wiped up some splashes from the table with the towel and put the bottle back into the silvery bucket. "Phew," she said, before picking up a box of her favourite choccies, which she'd brought with her, and then walking out onto the balcony and sitting down. I followed and plopped down not far from the doorway - no way was I going near the edge! The sun was still shining and we were about to depart; our holiday was really beginning now!

We sat there for a while, me savouring the late afternoon sunshine and Sheila sipping her drink and nibbling at her choccies - I noticed that she ate four! She looked at her time-telling machine. "Any minute now, Truffles," she remarked. And, indeed, just after she spoke there was a very, very loud noise from the ship (I thought it sounded like a pack of lions all roaring in unison), and she got up and leaned on the glass edge wall of the balcony, looking over the side. I remained where I was - I felt safer there.

Sheila was talking to the neighbours and they were chinking their glasses and telling each other what a lovely time they were going to have and saying how lucky they were to be on such a beautiful ship. It was going to be a real treat for them all to be pampered, entertained and fed to the highest standard, and most definitely worth it even though it had cost them an arm and a leg. An arm and a leg? What did they mean by that? I wondered. I thought you humans paid for things with that stuff called money (or dosh, lolly, spondulicks, as I've also heard you refer to it!) But surely you don't chop off your arms and legs to buy things? Sheila's remained intact, so obviously she paid for the holiday some other way. I was puzzled yet again by the odd things you humans come out with! Still, I wasn't going to do my head in worrying about it. I was feeling much too relaxed to bother.

I couldn't even feel we were moving. But from the others' conversation I gathered that we were now away from the dockside and leaving Southampton. Sheila sat back down again, resisted the temptation of another choccy and sipped some more bubbly. "This is the life, Truffles," she said. I agreed - to sit lazing in the sun and dozing all day, only really having to move to eat your meals, was most definitely my idea of heaven!

I knew that Sheila's idea of heaven was to be on a cruise ship, particularly this one. She had been with this cruise line many times before. If circumstances permitted, I reckon she would go on it about six times a year instead of two! I have heard her telling some friends who have never been on cruises that they really ought to try one. Even though they had probably seen pictures, both still and moving, it was impossible to understand just how big a cruise ship was until you were stood by its side looking up and feeling dizzy! And inside (well, on this particular cruise line anyway) it was just pure, unadulterated luxury - like a big floating hotel with every amenity you could want. Her friends had remained unconvinced - well, it was their loss!

We sat out for an hour or so, and then I stood up, looking upwards and outwards - though I still hadn't plucked up the courage to go right to the outer edge - and I could see that the many large surrounding buildings of the port had now vanished and in the distance, just past the water, was some green countryside with just a few low buildings here and there. I could see now that we were definitely moving, as the scenery was changing all the time, but we weren't going nearly as fast as we did in Tony's motor machine, not by a long chalk. Perhaps I would like this better - this more civilised and genteel way of moving.

Sheila checked her time-keeping gadget and gathered up her glass and the choccy box. Then she said the magic words: "Time for your dinner, Truffles!" That's more like it, I thought. "It's lovely, so you can eat outside," she said, "and then you won't make any mess on the carpet either." What a cheek, I thought - I never make a mess on the carpet. My manners are far too good for that! I waited impatiently and she brought me out a bowl of my favourite chicken and turkey in gravy topped with a healthy sprinkling of crunchy biscuits. I eat this a lot of the time at home, but I was hoping that on this cruise I would have the chance to sample perhaps some more exotic foods! By the time Sheila turned round after one more look over the balcony edge, the meal had gone - I was that hungry! We both came back into the stateroom and she pulled the sliding glass doors together, leaving just a small opening for me to squeeze through for access to my litter box. Might as well go now as later, I thought, so out I went out again and had a nice sit down followed by a bit of digging and scratching. I returned inside and indicated that I had finished and that she should forget she was on holiday for a moment and concentrate on her toilet cleaning duties pour moi! I didn't have to worry. "Oh good, you've been," she said. "I must tidy it all away, as I don't want Eduardo to find anything nasty when he comes in later. I'll have to keep an eye on your box. Lucky you went now, because I don't want to be cleaning it out when I'm all dressed up for my own dinner!" She busied herself sorting out the box and I retired onto my fluffy bed, where I enjoyed a calming licking session followed by a pleasant scratch. I was beginning to feel quite drowsy - it must have been the sea air!

# The first evening on board

Whilst I dozed on and off I could hear Sheila rummaging around the cupboards and laying out some of her outer coverings on the bed. She switched on the wall picture-making machine and sat and watched it for a while before disappearing to carry out her ablutions and then reappearing to change into her outfit for the evening. She then spent what seemed to me to be an extraordinarily long time fussing about her face and head fur before she finally gazed into the looking glass and said, "Well, that's about the best I can do." She took out something sparkly from a drawer and clipped it round her neck and then went to the little cupboard with the inner heavy door, pressed some of its buttons and stuck more sparkly bits on her paws. I blinked. I'd never seen her so 'dressed up' at home. She looked very different somehow. Quite nice! Maybe this was what dressing for an evening on a cruise ship did to you - made you smarten yourself up more. Not that (I hasten to say, as she will be reading this) she ever looks sloppy. She is not a 'casual' type of person. Although we live in the countryside, she is a town girl at heart and never goes out without everything matching, head fur tidy or covered with a snazzy hat, paw covers and handbags colour-coordinated, etc. - you get the picture. On a cruise she can really go to town and that's why she takes so much luggage. Most things will only see the light of day once and then will be packed away again - what an exhausting business, I thought, and all for vanity! Still, if it keeps her happy ...

"Now, Truffles," she said, "Time for me to go for a pre-dinner cocktail and then to the dining room to meet my tablemates for the cruise. You will be quite okay here - have a nice sleep, and Eduardo will come in soon I expect." I knew what dinner was, of course, but what on earth was a cocktail - something that hangs on the rear end of a chicken? I like birds' tails, but somehow I couldn't imagine that they would appeal to Sheila very much. Perhaps they are a delicacy you humans just have on board ships - ah yes, maybe they are seagulls' tails?

She patted me, took a small bottle off the top of the drawer units and sprayed some sickly smelling stuff from it on her neck, then glanced in the looking glass once more and went out, closing the stateroom door behind her. I settled down again and almost immediately fell asleep.

I don't know how long I slept, but I was awoken by a light knock at the door and a voice outside saying something I thought sounded like "housekeeping". I sat up. The door opened and I got ready to retreat to my safe spot behind the bed. But it was Eduardo - that was okay, he was nice, I liked him. "'Ello Trufools," he said, then bent down and gave me a pat. "'Ow are you, leetle puzzy?" He talked in a funny human way, not like Sheila does or, indeed, any of her Cornish friends, who also seem to have a different accent from hers. I remember her saying once that she came from a place called Surrey, which I don't think is in Cornwall or even nearby to it. Cats speak in different tongues, too, you know. For example, when I was living in our home near the fields (where I told you I occasionally used to hear gunshot bangs) one of my old feline pals there was Taro, who was a Birman but who had been born in some other place called Liverpool, and he had a very unique miaow that was scouse/oriental! The other cats' accents were mostly Cornish or Devonian, with one exception, who also came from 'up north' somewhere! I always found it difficult to understand Taro, especially when we had one of our cat slanging matches and his voice got shriller and shriller with rage. Probably just as well, because if I'd understood the words he was hurling at me, no doubt I would have blushed with embarrassment! He was a very feisty character! I sometimes remember my past housemates and wish they were still with us. We were all shapes and sizes - five or six cats, a Basset hound, a St Bernard and a Macaw parrot, plus various indoor and outdoor fish. Something for all tastes - fur, fish and feather, Sheila used to say! You can read all about them and the funny things that happened to us in my diaries.

Eduardo patted me for a few moments and then said, "I 'av sometheeng for you, Trufools," and he reached into his pocket (yes, another person who has a pocket - why can't I have one?) and brought out something wrapped in shiny tra... trans... transp... clear paper. It was a lovely little silvery fish. Ooh, I thought, that looks tasty - and it was! I rubbed round his legs, showing my pleasure. What a nice man! I sat in my bed again and watched Eduardo bustling about, changing Sheila's drinking glasses, polishing the big looking glass, pulling the curtains over the balcony doors and doing things in the ablution room. Finally he turned down her big bed and put a choccy on the pillow (ooh, she'll love that, I thought) and then he brought over a towel and began folding it and folding it until eventually, I thought, it looked to be in the shape of a dog, or maybe a lion, I wasn't sure. He placed it on the bed together with another of those printed paper sheets. "Goodnight, Trufools," he said, and then he slipped out of the door, leaving some wall lights on above the bed that gave a cosy glow to the room.

Once he'd gone, I nipped up on the bed and took the opportunity to flex my claws on the soft towel. A lovely feeling! I trod and trod on the lovely fluffy material for nearly five minutes and the image of the dog or lion or whatever it was swiftly disappeared. I don't know why Sheila was so cross earlier when she'd seen me doing it in the ablution room. After all, there were about ten towels in there, so surely she wasn't going to use them all! Oh well, if Eduardo was going to leave a towel on the bed each night specially for me, I would have to leave my daily flexing exercises until then - it didn't really matter to me at what time of day I did them. Anything to keep the peace! I went back to my own bed and decided to have a nice doze. The little fish would get itself digested and my batteries would get recharged.

Quite some time must have elapsed when I heard the door opening again, this time without a warning knock. The main light came on and Sheila appeared. I stretched and sat up. "Well, Truffles," she said, "I've had a really good dinner and the people at my table are ever so nice. I'm just going to the loo and wash my hands and then I'll take you for a bit of a stroll round the ship. I'm not going to have a late night tonight, I'm feeling quite tired after our early start this morning." Well, me too - it had been a long day. She disappeared into the ablution room and once again I heard that horrendous flushing noise. I would get used to that in a day or so and take no notice I expect.

Out she came and she walked over to the bed. She paused by the crumpled towel, looking puzzled. "I've seen better efforts at towel folding in a kids' playgroup," she remarked. Then she looked hard at me. "Was this YOU, Truffles?" she said. "I'm sure Eduardo wouldn't leave it in a state like this!" I said nothing and hung my head. I didn't want to get Eduardo into trouble, as he was such a nice man. "Oh well, never mind now," said Sheila. "Where's your lead? Let's go."

We sauntered along the passageway and came to the bank of

elevators. Sheila pressed a button on the wall and soon one arrived, heralded by the ghostly female human voice saying, "Doors opening". Inside it didn't seem quite so scary as it had done the first time I'd seen it, and I courageously walked towards the outer edge and peered through the glass as we hurtled down towards the lower decks. We passed some real, yes real, trees that appeared to be su... sus... susp... hung up in big round buckets in the air and all around I could see beautiful pictures and statue things. It was totally mind-boggling to me. Sheila was admiring the view but didn't seem particularly gobsmacked herself. Then I remembered, of course, she had been on this ship before, so it wasn't new to her. The elevator stopped and, as we were exiting an elderly male passenger got in, doing something of a double-take as he noticed me. "Well, I've seen pink elephants when I've had a few," he spluttered, "but never a tabby cat!" I watched him shaking his head as the doors closed.

Sheila tugged on my lead and we walked out of the elevator area. In front of us I saw a kind of floor made of glass with coloured lights shining up through it. Fascinating! As we neared it I realised it was actually a glass bridge leading to a street and there were lots of people walking up and down it, looking at the shops and other places on each side of it. It was just like a town. But how can you have a town inside a ship, I asked myself? Something else for my frazzled brain to attempt to solve! Sheila regularly goes to our nearest big town in Cornwall, so she once explained to me exactly what a 'town' is. She usually visits one near us called Truro and she told me that it is full of these shop places where you humans like to spend your money. Humans and their use of money are still a puzzling scenario to me - if you all want this thing called money so very much, why on earth, when you DO get it, do you then go out and get rid of it? I know that Sheila always says she can "shop for England" (especially when she is on a cruise ship or ashore in some other country!) and as soon as she ever seems to get any money it never lasts very long! "Well, you can't take it with you," is something she's often said, too, or, "There's no pockets in shrouds!" I'm not sure exactly what a shroud is, but she doesn't seem to want one. But there, see, perhaps these shrouds are like cats: they don't have desirable pockets either!

As we crossed over the glass bridge I kept looking down between my paws, wondering where the lovely colours were coming from that were shining up through it. Perhaps there was a rainbow underneath it? Isn't there a song you sing about a yellow brick road leading to a rainbow? Well, this definitely wasn't made of yellow bricks; it was glass. I've sometimes seen rainbows in the sky when I've been in our garden. Don't tell me there was a garden inside this ship, too? Though, after what I'd already seen today, nothing would surprise me any more! All of this was like being in a dream - totally incomprehensible (another word from the human vocabulary I'm proud to know the meaning of!) to a little cat like me.

We ambled slowly along the road, passing lots of people who either stopped and said, "Hello, puss," or laughed as they walked by. I ignored the laughter and decided not to let it bother me. I don't think it was meant to be unkind laughter anyway; more probably they were all rather taken aback at seeing a cat on board and didn't really know what to say or do. So I smiled at them all and purred on demand if someone patted me. I would need to get Sheila to brush my fur when we got back, after being patted by so many strange, sweaty paws. Normally I don't like anybody I'm not familiar with to touch me - I'm very particular about hygiene!

As we passed the shops, Sheila was telling me about them. The first one was the coffee shop, where you humans love to drink that hot and frothy brown stuff. I know she loves her coffee, but of course she couldn't go inside just then as I was with her, unfortunately. We continued on past a general store with shelves full of those coloured drink bottles, boxes of choccies and all manner of other things. Next were several more shops containing all kinds of your outer coverings, hats and handbags, the sparkly things for your paws, printed papers, luggage and toys for infant humans. I noticed some very realistic furry creatures for the infants - dogs and cats, fishes, meerkats and lots of teddy bears. Now, Sheila has a large collection of teddy bears and she usually brings one home from every ship she travels on. She's bound to spend some of her money on one of them from this shop, I thought! Her 'travelling bears' all sit together on a large armchair in her bedroom. Most of them wear vests with ships' names on them, so she can look at them and treasure the memories they bring of past cruises, I suppose. Bit pathetic, I've always thought, but whatever turns you on!

Talking of teddy bears, as we walked on I glanced to the right and saw a rather snazzy, sporty, bright blue motor machine parked on the road outside one of the places where you drink those naughty drinks. Surely they can't drive motor machines *inside* the ship? I thought! It looked real enough, though it didn't actually seem as if it was going to move anywhere. I blinked and looked again, this time noticing that the driver was, in fact, a huge teddy bear, with another one sitting beside him! Both were attired in smart navy blue tops with the name of the ship on the front. People were milling around them, taking pictures on their little picture gadgets or their flat speaking machines. They certainly seemed very popular - even more than me! Sheila looked, too. "Pity I can't carry you home," she said laughing. Just as well, I thought - God alone knows where you'd put them!

We carried on past another drinking place called the Dog and Badger - should have been called The Cat and Fiddle, I reckon! A much more popular name, surely! Then on to yet more ladies' outer covering shops before we finally reached the end of the road. "Right, Truffles," said Sheila, "we'll go down the other side of the parade now and then make our way back to the stateroom. It's 11 o'clock and we both need our beauty sleep after such a long day." Speak for yourself, I thought, I'm beautiful enough - but I did agree that some proper sleep would be nice!

We passed a foreign eating and drinking place where Sheila said they sold pizzas (I didn't have the least idea what a pizza was, but she didn't explain!) and then we were at the drinking place with the bears in their motor machine parked outside. It also looked foreign, with lots of tall, thin bottles with unpronounceable names on them. Next we came to a shop with a horrible, sickly smell coming from it. My whiskers twitched in disgust and I felt like throwing up, but Sheila dragged me in a little way and picked up one or two small containers, spraying some of their sweet-smelling contents on her paw. "Mmmm, I must get some of this tomorrow," she said. Well don't put any of it on me, I thought. Once outside I took a deep breath - that was better! I understood now what the shop was selling - the stuff she puts on her neck before she goes out. Well, okay in small quantities, I conceded, but ugh, I don't want to go in there again sniffing gallons of the stuff! Next we arrived at a shop full of sparkly things and little time-keeping machines. "Better not look in there now," she said. "It'll be too tempting." Oh yes, I've heard that before, I thought. Now we arrived at a place that I did think looked good - an ice cream shop. I like ice cream; in fact, I like any kind of cream - single, double, whipped and, most especially, Cornish clotted! No chance for me here, I supposed crossly - with the Elf and Safety rules. As if she read my thoughts, Sheila smiled down at me and said, "When we're somewhere ashore, Truffles, I'll buy you an ice cream. Italian ice cream tastes even better than Cornish ice cream!" I couldn't believe that, but decided to reserve judgement. The ice cream shop I noticed was called Ben and Jerry's - there again, a better title would have been Tom and Jerry's, wouldn't it? Obviously the people who named the shops on this ship were not very cat orientated: *Dog* and Badger, and *Ben* is a popular dog's name!

Next to the ice cream shop (though Sheila called it a parlour, for some obscure reason!) was a narrow shop where male humans could have fur shaved off their cheeks and the fur on top of their heads cut short. What for? A cat would never, ever have its fur cut off! Our fur is our most prized asset and is what attracts those opposite members of the feline sex as well as our human carers to us. I cannot understand why male humans don't want to let their fur and whiskers grow normally! Wouldn't female humans find them more attractive in their natural state? Obviously not, for whatever reason - but I'll never understand it. But then, no cat will ever understand the human vagaries of life, and certainly no human will ever understand cats!

Finally we came to the last shop, which contained more outer coverings but of a sporty nature. Sheila wouldn't be tempted by anything in there - she's certainly not sporty! She's always said the only exercise she gets is walking around shops! Then it was back over the rainbow-coloured bridge again, and to the elevator bank. In we got and up we rose, and then it was the long trudge right to the back of the ship and our comfy stateroom. I think perhaps Sheila was regretting choosing a room so far away. But there again, I thought, the long trek back and forth several times a day would be excellent exercise for her, which could only be good for her thighs!

Once inside the stateroom, she locked the door and slid open the balcony doors for me to perform my night-time ablutions in the litter box whilst she performed her own in the inner ablution room - 'bathroom', I think I heard Eduardo call it when they were talking earlier, so I must remember to refer to it as that now, I suppose. Not that I could see a bath in it!

Whilst I sat and had my last lick-over of the day, she busied herself putting away all her stuff. I noticed her glance again at the incriminating towel lying on the bed. Oh dear, I thought, here it comes! "Now look here, Truffles," she said, "I know that Eduardo would never have left a scrunched-up towel behind. The service on this ship is far too good for a thing like that to happen. And I bet he had made it into a lovely animal or something for me - that's what the stewards do at bedtime. It's a bit of fun for us - and you've totally ruined it! Now DON'T do it again or I'll tell Eduardo and he'll be very upset with you!" Well, I didn't want to upset Eduardo, really I didn't, because I was looking forward to the treats I hoped he'd be bringing me each day! And he was a very pleasant human, as humans go. So I hung my head and rubbed around her ankles, looking up with what I hoped was a sorrowful expression. "Oh, go on with you," she said, picking me up and stroking me and giving me a kiss. "I'll forgive you. You didn't understand." So amicable relations between us were resumed and I gave up my dream of towel-flexing each day! It wasn't worth upsetting the apple cart (as you humans say - I would have used the term fish wagon).

We both got into our respective beds, she turned out the lights and before I fell almost instantly into a deep and dreamless sleep

I just had time to reflect on the things that had stuck most in my mind about this wonderful day. I had never seen so many doors, never seen so much glass, and certainly never seen so many humans in one place before! What would tomorrow bring?

# First day at sea

The sun filtering through a gap in the curtains woke us both up. Sheila glanced at the time-telling machine beside her bed and got up, slipping into a trendy white towelling dressing robe with the ship's name on its pocket (Yes, even that humble robe had a pocket!) with matching paw covers to complete her early morning ensemble. She opened the balcony doors and blinked in the bright sunlight. Me too! It seemed much more powerful than we get at home - maybe it was reflecting back from the great big silvery blue C that surrounded us. There again, at home the sun usually puts his hat on! I padded out and carried out my early morning business in the litter box and then, growing very daring, eased my way towards the outer edge of the balcony. I peeped out through the glass and this time I didn't feel nearly so wobbly - perhaps it was not going to be so scary after all, I thought. I had known I would get used to the balcony in time. It was only because this whole ship experience was so very new and alien to a little cat like me, and, in the space of only a few hours, I had seen just so many new things I could never, ever have imagined in a million years! I am not a scaredy-cat as a rule (apart from when I hear those giant birds you ride in going over in the sky and making such a roaring noise), so I resolved that I would not let anything else I came across on the ship frighten me. After all, I reasoned to myself, Sheila would be with me all the time and I knew she wouldn't let anything bad happen to me. I felt much more cheerful and positive and went back inside to chivvy up my breakfast.

Looking at the big blue C!

After Sheila had been in the bathroom, dressed herself, seen to her head fur and given mine my daily brush, I ate a nice bowl of haddock pâté with crunchies, and settled down in a sunny corner of the balcony to wash my whiskers and rid them of the fishy smell. Sheila carried out her litter box cleaning duties and I gave a nod to tell her I was satisfied with its now pristine appearance. Neither of us wanted Eduardo to see a used litter box!

"Right," she said, "I'm off for my own breakfast now, so see you later. Then we'll go for a walk outside." Outside? OUTSIDE? How can we go outside? I wondered - we'll fall off into the C! Oh no, no, no! Come on, Truffles, I chided myself sternly, you said you'd not get frightened anymore, so trust in Sheila - everything will be okay. So I looked up at her and continued with the whisker cleaning. She disappeared out of the stateroom and I returned to the sunny balcony and dozed ...

Some time later, in came Eduardo. "'Ello, Trufools," he said, coming outside and patting me. "'Ow are you today?" I smarmed round his legs purring, hoping that he would give me some tasty titbit - and I wasn't disappointed! "'Ere you are, puss," and he bent down and gave me a little dish of tuna flakes, which were really nice. I'm well in here, I thought! I sat back whilst he cleaned the entire stateroom and bathroom literally from top to bottom, changing all the sheets on Sheila's bed (I didn't have any sheets on mine!) and replacing used towels and drinking glasses. Fortunately, he never made any comment when he found the results of my efforts on his towelling dog, but I have to admit that a twinge of guilt did run through me. He refilled the fruit bowl and the ice bucket, where Sheila's unfinished bottle of bubbly still sat, and gave the flowers a drink. Then, job done, he gave me a farewell pat and vanished.

It must have been about mid-morning when Sheila reappeared. She must have enjoyed a really big breakfast, I thought, after she'd deafened me again with the horrendous flushing system on this ship! She rummaged around in the drawer she'd allocated to the storage of my collars, brushes and bits and pieces and found a rather smart nautical navy and white leather collar decorated with little anchors that she'd bought me specially for the trip. I'd thought it rather naff at the time, but having seen the senior crew members (hossifers - is that what you call them?) looking 'rather dishy', as Sheila put it, in the same colour scheme, I changed my mind. It kind of went with the ship. Matching lead attached, off we set.

After the usual long trek to where the elevators lived, we didn't have long to wait until one arrived with the mysterious female human's usual welcome and warning that she was closing the doors. I did wonder exactly where this lady hung out - hopefully I might find out before the end of the cruise. It was niggling me! She must be very busy, I mused - there were so many elevators and I reckoned I'd not seen half of them yet. Perhaps she buzzed about more rapidly than the speed of light from one to another as they each arrived at the different levels - so fast that nobody could see her. But I would never know, so I gave up worrying about it!

After a few moments we arrived at the top deck of the ship, where there were more glass sliding doors leading out on to what seemed to be a huge kind of walking and sitting area for the passengers. I thought I could see some big water pools in the distance, too. Sheila tugged at my lead. "Come on," she said, "we'll walk right around the edge of the deck, all round the ship from end to end." We strolled along slowly and I was so busy looking all about me that I didn't really bother that, once more, people were looking at me and some were laughing. There seemed to be hundreds and hundreds of people, of all shapes and sizes, lounging on low chairs nearly all dressed in not altogether flattering outer coverings. In fact, I had never seen so many fat people dressed in such small coverings - hardly decent, I would have said! I know that in public Sheila never likes to show fellow humans her legs with, of course, 'those' thighs! I suspected that when she wanted to do a bit of sun worshipping she would do it in the seclusion of our own balcony. Quite right, too, I thought - we don't want other people's holidays being spoilt by the sight of her in a partly undressed state! In any case, over the years she has never gone a nice light brown colour (which is what she's aimed for) when she's been sitting out in the sun. She always goes a rather nasty shade of red, which is not in the least bit attractive! Of course I, on the other paw (sorry, hand, I think you say) have a coat that is already in a very nice colour combination of light browns and tans, so there's no need for me to worry about getting a tan in the sun - I already have one!

After a short walk we arrived at one of the water pools I had spotted. Several people were in the water, floating about or swimming. What were they - masochists? What a horrible experience being dowsed all over in water. I shuddered. Mind you, they seemed to be enjoying it. Nevertheless, I would make sure I kept well away from the edge. I didn't fancy getting splashed!  Sheila noticed my 'full of trepidation' look. She laughed. "You ain't seen nothing yet, Truffles!" We continued on and then she stopped by a couple of people, who were apparently her dining table companions. They greeted me with pats and I gave the obligatory purr. They suggested that we sit with them for a few minutes, so Sheila drew up a chair and I lay underneath it. They were talking about the wonderful food they'd had the night before and also at breakfast. All agreed that they had never seen so much choice of food and of such a high standard. No wonder there were so many fat people about, I thought!

"I must tell you something funny," the lady said. Her name was Dianne and her husband was called David. She went on, "You remember the very fat family we noticed yesterday evening? The mother and father were both well over thirty stone and their teenage kids were at least eighteen stone each and I nicknamed them the 'Golightly' family." Sheila nodded. David smiled. "I thought they were probably members of the 18-30 Holiday Club," he remarked. "Stones, that is, not age groups!" They all giggled. "Well," continued Dianne, "when we went to get into the elevator before breakfast, Mr and Mrs Golightly were already in it, together with the two children. Although the elevator was supposed to take up to twenty people, there was just no room in it for anyone else at all, so we had to wait for the next one. Anyway, later in the breakfast buffet we were sitting at our table and we saw Mr Golightly lumbering back from the food bar, carrying in one hand an enormous dinner plate heaped up with crispy bacon rashers - the mound was about the size of a large Christmas pudding that would have fed twelve people! In the other hand he was balancing an equally large plate loaded with so many slices of toast that it probably amounted to an entire loaf of bread! We thought, oh that's nice, he's collecting breakfast for the family! But no, waddling behind him came Mrs Golightly, and she was carrying exactly the same!" "No!" gasped Sheila. "Yes," said Dianne, "So they were obviously just carrying their *own* breakfasts. And, what's more, behind them along followed the kids, and each one of them was carrying an equally large plate with no less than three gigantic cheeseburgers on it!" "Well, no wonder they are the size they are," said Sheila, "I know I eat too much when I'm on a ship, but not to that extreme, thank goodness! If I meet Mrs Golightly anywhere, I'll have to go and stand beside her, then I'll feel quite slim!" They all laughed again, but I felt a bit nauseous - we cats never eat too much (dogs tend to do so though!) as we know how to keep ourselves healthy and being overweight is not good, nor is it for humans I would have thought. "Of course, because we tend to eat so much more on holiday, you've heard the old saying on board a cruise ship haven't you?" said Sheila. "You go on board as a passenger and go off as cargo!" They all laughed again. Sheila got up, saying that she would see them in the evening - 'formal night' she called it. I got another pat from Dianne and David and we progressed on our ship's tour.

On and on we strolled - the deck seemed never-ending. Suddenly we came to a large expanse of real grass, yes readers, REAL grass! I couldn't believe it, but I walked onto it and, yes, it was definitely real and, what's more, it was also growing and it felt lovely underneath my paws. I looked up at Sheila. "Yes, Truffles," she said, "real grass! We'll come here again tomorrow and you can sit on it for a bit in the sun. You'll think you're back in the garden again." Our garden isn't as big as this, I thought, more's the pity. At our previous house we did have a very large garden indeed and I've always thought it was a shame to leave it, but apparently it took a lot of work to keep it going. I could see people playing with sets of balls, rolling them along one after another, and there were others holding what looked to me like big wooden hammers and knocking coloured wooden balls through hoops. Come to think of it, people played the ball and hoop game on our grass at our previous home. The wooden hammers (I've just remembered that Sheila used to refer to them as mallets) came in a long wooden box that I used to like hiding away in when I was younger! Past memories, eh! Well, it would certainly be far better to spend time here than by that awful water pool, I thought. What a lovely place! I was looking forward to tomorrow already!

On we walked, past another water pool with lots of coloured water jets spouting over it, and then found ourselves alongside a long room with big glass windows (glass, glass and ever more glass on this ship!) Sheila stopped and peered through the windows. As they reached right down to the ground I was able to peek through them, too. I could see lots of people walking on the spot on some kind of moving roads, but they weren't getting anywhere. Strange! There were others sitting on two-wheeled contraptions, with their paws sitting on small blocks that were going round and round, making the big wheels turn very fast but, again, they weren't moving from the spot. Even stranger! The people seemed to be putting a great deal of effort into it all, as they were sweating buckets (a charming little saying of yours, I believe), but it all appeared to be for nothing as they were going nowhere. What a strange pastime, I thought. We cats climb trees, chase mice and jump up and over fences to get our exercise, so at least we do move about; I would get very frustrated if I was just jumping up and down and not getting anywhere. As I've remarked before, cats and humans have such very different priorities! Sheila lingered for a few moments, appreciatively watching some young male humans who were raising and lowering their rather hefty arms and holding things that looked like giant egg timers in their paws, which seemed to be very heavy.

Then we set off again, and finally, yes finally, we reached the end of the decking road and the front of the ship. Although the sun was still very bright and hot it was very windy here. I felt that if I had not been anchored to the lead I might have flown away! Still, that would have been an uplifting (excuse the pun!) experience for a cat. How wonderful it would be, I thought, to fly like a bird - and how much easier it would be to catch one! One can dream, I suppose ...

Sheila leaned forward into the buffeting wind and, dragging me behind, crossed the width of the ship and turned round the corner, where the walking route continued back in the direction we had come from. We passed the other side of the room where the people were still frantically running and jumping, etc., and then arrived back at the grassy area once more. Two people were playing the ball and hoop game and Sheila stopped to watch them. "Do you play?" the lady asked. Sheila told her that she did but hadn't done for some time. "Oh well, join us for a game tomorrow," smiled the lady. "My name's Connie and this is my husband Ron. And who is this you have with you?" she said, smiling down at me and giving me a pat on the head. She seemed nice, so I smiled back. Sheila told them about me and how I'd come to be on the ship, and they all agreed to have a game the next morning. I would be able to sit and watch them on the lovely grass, too.

We continued our stroll and next we passed by a rather frightening - to me - place where lots of people were watching several pretty lady crew members, who seemed to be showing them how to make glass (yes - I was definitely beginning to get paranoid about seeing all the glass on this ship and I certainly didn't want to watch it being made as well!) objects in many different colours. It was fiery and there were hissing noises that I didn't like. They had long glass tubes in their mouths with hot, runny blobs on the end of them, and it looked as if they were blowing air down these tubes. Sheila walked on by pretty quickly, for which I was grateful. She realised that I would not like this particular place. I have to say that she is very conscientious about her duties as my carer and does perform these to a very high standard. It's very rare that I have to chastise her, and after all the years we've been together she knows exactly how my mind works. I expect she will go on her own and watch it all at another time.

Eventually we reached the entrance doors and wended our way to the elevators. Then it was back to the stateroom. Sheila opened up the balcony and I went out and sat in my sunny corner. "Well, that was a nice stroll to work off my big breakfast," she said. "I think I'll go and have a cup of coffee in that nice sophisticated café and gelateria on the upper shopping floor. I might have a mooch around the shops, too. You'll be okay here, Truffles." Mmmm ... yes, I would - nothing like a peaceful doze in the sun. I turned round a couple of times and went into sleep mode.

Sometime later I awoke and went to look out over the edge of the balcony again: C, nothing but C all around, wherever I looked. In one way it was frightening and intimidating to be surrounded by all that nasty water - a cat's nightmare - and it looked hellishly deep, too, but on the other hand it was a pretty awesome sight. I wondered what my past pussy pals - Taro, Tansy, Lucky and Robbie - would have made of it. They would have been as baffled as I was, I expect. In our previous big garden we'd had a large pond, which could even have been described as a small lake depending on how you looked at it, but we weren't overawed or frightened by it; in fact, we used to like it, as lots of fish lived in it and we enjoyed watching them from its banks. It would never have entered our heads to venture into the water, although I do remember that little Tansy (who was always in trouble!) fell into it a few times. Pretty scary! Shaking my head at it all, I went and had a drink of the stuff from the bowl Sheila had put out and lay back down again.

A few minutes went by and then Sheila arrived back, carrying a paper bag from which she took out a sparkly evening handbag. Not another one, I thought! "This is nice, isn't it Truffles," she said. "I just couldn't resist it." She reached into the big cupboard and brought out a pair of her paw covers. "Just right," she said. "I knew they'd match! Tonight is 'formal night', so I'll have the chance to really dress up!" I wondered what a 'formal night' was, but she wasn't forthcoming. Another mystery, I supposed, but whatever it was I now knew you had to look extra smart for it. We sat outside for a while and then Sheila gave me my lunchtime snack of crunchies and went off to have her own. I went back to sleep ...

Eventually Sheila returned and she joined me outside, where we sat companionably for a while basking in the warm sunshine. Sheila had said earlier that we would be seeing even hotter sun later on in our travels, so I was well looking forward to that! The hotter the better for me! "Right," she said, "come on, we'll go for another walk outside and I'll show you something you'll really like!" My curiosity was getting the better of me now - well, you do know how curious we cats are, don't you? On with the lead and off we went.

This time the unseen lady in the elevator announced a different deck from the one we'd walked around yesterday and it seemed even higher up! We started our promenade around the outside decking track and passed another water pool that was for human kittens ('children' is your formal word, but I always think of youngsters as 'kittens'). There were lots of them playing and darting in and out of the water, and all around were large coloured balls, climbing frames, pool toys and more of those shooting water spouts. They looked to be having lots of fun but, as I said earlier, it would be a horrific place for any cat's kitten to play in. A sandpit would be much more preferable! This ship obviously had every amenity you could think of, so I expect there was sandpit somewhere, too!

We continued past a multitude of chairs with hundreds of people sitting on them and enjoying the sun. I must say, where we live in Cornwall, the sun had been a bit scarce recently, so I supposed everyone was making the most of it - not that I could believe they all came from Cornwall. I now knew of the place called Southampton, so perhaps everyone else lived there. On we walked, past another water pool (how many have they got on this ship? I wondered - not content with being surrounded by the stuff, they want bits of it inside, too!) Then we arrived at an open space with more chairs around it, and I gasped. What was this ahead - a mountain?

Sheila chuckled. "I said I had a nice surprise for you," she said. "Perhaps you can go climbing now!" The mountain had lots of small holes and ledges all the way up it and there were two man passengers wearing round hard-looking hats on their heads, with straps around their bodies attached to long ropes, who were attempting to climb up to the top of the thing - and not making a very good job of it either! Obviously neither of them had a clue what they were doing. We cats are the worldwide experts in that field (except for a small pr... pro... propor... a few that let the side down when they get stuck up trees or lamp posts). I could show them a thing or two, I thought. I looked expectantly at Sheila and then up towards the mountain. She turned to a fit-looking young male crew member who was standing nearby and looking curiously at me. After the usual explanation about my reason for being on the ship, he bent down and patted me. The way Sheila was looking at him, I reckoned she would have liked him to pat her, too! "Would you let Truffles have a climb?" she asked. "Well, madam," he replied, "I'm not sure. Would a little cat like that be able to climb all the way up there? We wouldn't want her to fall off and I don't have any safety equipment that would fit a cat - we don't have a lot of cats booking cruises with this line!" Sarcastic so-and-so, I thought. His attitude made me all the more determined to climb the mountain, which I knew would be easy-peasy for me. That would show him! After listening for a few moments longer to him going on about his friends the Elf and Safety people, I thought, blow it, and jerked the lead out of Sheila's hand. "Hold on a minute, Truffles," she cried. No way, I muttered to myself, and I ran over to the mountain.

As I thought, it was a dead simple climb for any reasonably competent cat. There were so many of those small holes and ledges that I just sprang from one to another with hardly any effort. I soon passed the two struggling climbers, one of whom nearly lost his footing and had to hold on to the rope with both paws when he saw me going by. Fortunately, he didn't fall - that would have made me feel a bit guilty! You humans just don't have the landing skills that we cats have. "Hey, Bob," he shouted to his friend, "am I hallucinating or what? Did a cat just pass us by?" His friend, dumbstruck, made no reply, but at least he didn't miss his step! I smiled to myself, waved my tail at them and carried on, paw over paw, until I was right at the top, where there was a piece of cloth attached to a stick waving in the wind next to a large bell. At this height the wind was very strong indeed and I must admit that even I made sure my claws were firmly fixed into the mountain's top. I looked around me - what a view! I could see over the whole length of the ship from here. It was even longer than I had imagined. And when I turned round, right behind me I could see a large chimney - bigger than the one we have on our house, MUCH bigger! There was a cloud of white stuff coming from the chimney, but when it got up towards the sky it disappeared into the distance. All around me the sky was blue and the C underneath nearly matched it. I could hardly see where one started and one ended. Although hating water, and particularly C, it was a sight I would never forget as long as I lived. If I'd had any grandkittens it would have definitely been something to tell them. Unfortunately, after I was taken in by Sheila and family as a kitten myself they'd had some vital part removed from me, so no kittens were ever forthcoming!

I looked down, way down, and could see the two climbers still far behind me, struggling onwards and upwards (it would be dark before they got up here, I reckoned!) and the forms of Sheila and the crew member at the bottom, their arms waving at me and their mouths opening and closing, but I couldn't hear what they were saying. I expect they were calling me back down, but I decided I would stay on my perch for just a few more moments to savour this marvellous experience. I wouldn't delay my descent for too long, however, as I didn't want to get into hot water (pun!) again after the incident with the towels!

So I soon wended my way back down, which proved just as easy as going up really. As I passed climber Bob and his companion, he called out, "Hello, cat, wanna tell us how it's done?" Well, pal, I thought, just watch the expert and see what tips you can pick up! Finally at the bottom, I made my way back to Sheila. "Oh, Truffles, that was a bit naughty, rushing off like that," she said. "All sorts of things could have happened - still, all's well and I bet you enjoyed it, you little monkey!" The crew member laughed. "Well, I've seen it all now!" he said. After chatting to him for a few more minutes, Sheila tugged at the lead again and we walked away. "I knew you'd want to have a go," she said "but now you've done it, that's it. We were lucky that guy turned a blind eye and didn't stop you going up, as I'm sure it's probably not allowed!" Well, she needn't have worried, because my greatest pleasure really is just dozing in the sun in a quiet corner - so the balcony was my ideal, and I had no great ambition to stay outside on top of a mountain for too long in a howling gale. But I was pleased to have had the experience and I would savour the memory for quite a while.

THIS is how to do it!

A bit further on, Sheila decided that she'd get an ice cream. She stopped in front of a machine, pressed a button and directed a heap of the stuff, all swirly, into a container. Then she repeated the process using a smaller container. "And a bit for you, Truffles," she said. We moved away and she found an empty seat, sat down and started licking at her ice cream. I sat underneath and lapped mine up, too - yummy! When she'd finished, she stayed for a few more minutes chatting to the people beside her - the usual thing: how come a cat was with her? Then up we got and returned to the stateroom. I strolled out onto the balcony for a nap and she made herself a cup of the frothy stuff and switched on the moving-picture machine to watch the news. "I'll sit here for a while," she remarked, "because I should be getting my afternoon canapés delivered soon." I wondered what canapés were - maybe some sort of treat? Shortly afterwards, there came a knock at the door and a smiley steward (not Eduardo) arrived with a plate covered with a silver dome. Sheila thanked him and brought the plate out to the balcony table. Then she fetched herself a glass of the bubbly and sat down, removing the cover from the plate and revealing several of the aforesaid canapés! Yes, I sniffed appreciatively, they definitely were treats! Some were smoked salmon wrapped around little green things, others were prawns on little biscuits, and there were meaty treats and cheesy treats - all sorts. Sheila demolished a couple whilst sipping the bubbly. "Well, this is the life," she said, leaning back and half closing her eyes. "How the other half live!" I pawed her knee - couldn't I have a treat, too? "Too rich for you, Truffles," replied the mean so-and-so. I continued pawing her knee. "Oh, go on then," she said. "Here's one to try, but you won't like what's in the middle of it." Why not? I wondered. *She* seemed to like it. She dropped a little smoked salmon bundle down to me. Yes, it was nice; and no, I didn't like what was in the middle: as... asp... aspara... a green vegetable. Ugh, nice as the smoked salmon had been, I wouldn't have another one if I was offered it! I returned to my sunny corner and Sheila continued to sip and nibble.

When I woke up I saw that Sheila had disappeared into the bathroom and I could hear the sound of rushing water. When she emerged she rummaged through the cupboards and brought out some outer coverings, which she spread out on the bed. Oh yes, I thought, all her smartest stuff to wear on this 'formal night'. You know, I've never understood just why she has so many of these outer coverings, because she's always moaning about the washing and ironing of them. For me, a nice, well-fitting fur catsuit is suitable for all events and only needs a couple of lick-overs each day to keep it looking pristine - much more sensible!

"Now, Truffles," she said, "While I'm getting ready I think I'll order you a nice dinner to have here." She picked up a book that I'd noticed lying on the side, scanned through the pages and then went to the talking machine that was beside the bed and pressed a button. "Yes, I want to order some food - the poached salmon cutlet would be nice. Thank you." Yes, I thought, it most certainly *would* be nice.

Sheila had changed into her smart outfit and was just about to start fiddling about with her head fur when there was a knock at the door and a voice called, "Room service". "That was quick," said Sheila as she opened the door. The smiling steward who had delivered the canapés earlier came in, carrying a tray on which there was a covered plate. My nose twitched, as I could detect a rather delightful aroma coming from it. He set it down on the table and left, wishing Sheila "bon appetite", whatever that meant. Sheila took off the cover and - oh, heaven - I saw a lovely, thick pink piece of salmon surrounded by a creamy sauce that, to my sharp nose, smelt like prawn and cheese. I stood up on my back legs to reach the plate, but Sheila pushed me off. "Hang on a minute," she said. "Wait till I put it in your own bowl." "Hurry up then," I urged. Soon the transfer had been made and I was wolfing down the lovely salmon. If the food on this ship was going to be as good as this all the time, I would certainly be putting on extra weight, just like the rest of the passengers! I would become cat cargo! A few minutes later, re... rep... reple... full up, I settled down to my ritual after-dinner whisker wash.

Meanwhile, Sheila had been getting herself all dressed up and eventually, after at least another hour had gone by, I reckoned she seemed fairly satisfied with the final result. Well, she did look smart, I must say. The new bag she'd bought on the ship finished off her ensemble a treat. She was sparkling from top to toe! I just hoped the 'formal night' would prove to be all she had expected and that her dinner was as scrumptious as mine had been. I didn't think she would be choosing salmon, as for some odd reason she doesn't really like fish, but I've seen her eat prawns and lobster and crab, so I do know she likes them. She stroked me, glanced around the stateroom to check that all was tidy and then she left, saying when she got back later she would take me out for a walkabout again and maybe we'd go down to the casino, where perhaps I would bring her some luck! I wondered what a casino was and why she thought she'd need luck to go into it. Well, as I told you earlier, cats have always been supposed to be lucky, so yes, I hoped I would bring her luck. I retired to bed again and dozed, thinking of what a good day it had been and reflecting on all the new and interesting things I'd seen.

Later on I was awakened by Eduardo on his evening rounds. "'Ello, Trufools," he said, patting me. I purred back at him, and, although initially my game plan had been to be nice to him so that he would continue to bring me treats, it was no hardship purring and rubbing around his legs, as he was such a nice person anyway. I looked forward to seeing him, treat or no treat. However, in the event I wasn't disappointed, as he produced a few chopped pieces of grilled steak - and they were rather tasty, I can tell you! He busied himself around the stateroom and bathroom as usual. Pity Sheila is not so diligent in her household chores. She doesn't change all the sheets and towels every single day like he does. When he'd left, I noticed that his towelling creature this time was an elephant. Rather clever, I thought - Sheila will like that one! I went back to my bed ...

Sheila came back much later than on the previous night. I wondered where she'd been. As if she'd read my thoughts, she said, "Phew, what a marvellous dinner that was and then I went to the theatre after and the show was terrific - fabulous costumes, singing and dancing." Theatre, show, costumes? New words to me. I looked at her. "You won't know what I'm talking about, Truffles." she said. Try me. I thought. "A theatre is a place where lots of people go to watch a show, which is when other people dance and sing and do things they think will make the people watching happy and entertained. They wear colourful clothes, which they call costumes, and it all looks very exciting for the people watching; the group of people watching in a theatre are known as an audience. Don't bother about it, Truffles, you won't understand!" She laughed. Well, actually I *did* understand - I am much cleverer at fathoming out your human language than she thinks. Yes, I do get confused, because whilst we cats have one miaow sound for one thing and one for another and that never changes, in your speak several words often mean the same thing and just one word can mean several different things! I realise that what I've always called your 'outer coverings' are, in fact, known as clothes, but I don't like the word particularly, so that's why they will always be 'outer coverings' to me as a cat. Costume was obviously another word describing clothes, so that was something else to add to my ever-growing vocabulary! This trip was proving educational as well as enjoyable! What would be coming up next? I wondered.

Sheila opened my drawer and brought out my poshest collar and lead, made of golden coloured leather trimmed with diamanté. It tones beautifully with my tabby colouring. I remembered she'd brought it back from another cruise holiday. It seems there is a large chain of stores with big pet departments in some of the places where she gets off ships, and over the years she has brought me back lots of stuff - little packets of treats to eat that she cannot get me in Cornwall and some very snazzy neckwear, not to mention bedding and toys. She opened the little cupboard where she'd put her valuables and took out some of the money she had brought. So far I'd not seen her use any on the ship. I wonder why she wants it now, at this time of night?

Showing off the bling!

We walked the route to the elevators again and got in one, this time going downwards. When we got out I saw that we were on the floor under the coloured glass bridge, and we carried on past yet more places where people were drinking and enjoying themselves. Music was playing and there was a very happy atmosphere, I thought. Everyone looked very smart - nothing like as casual as they had been earlier in the day outside. The ladies were mostly in brightly coloured outer coverings with sparkly decorations on their arms and around their necks. They were tottering about on paw covers with those ridiculous high heels. I noticed that Sheila had removed hers when she'd got back to the stateroom and had replaced them with a lower-heeled pair. The men were dressed rather like those birds called penguins, I thought, generally in black and white. At one place we passed, people were dancing to some very lively foreign-sounding music that was being played by a group of four men wearing big straw hats, and Sheila explained to me that this was a Salsa Bar.

Eventually we arrived at an entrance with a sign 'CASINO' over it, leading to a huge room, which to me seemed crammed full of machines making jangling and clinking sounds and there were lots of people sitting either at these machines or else at tables where smartly dressed crew members - also looking rather like penguins - were entertaining groups of six or so people, all very intent on whatever game it was they were playing. I didn't want any long explanations from Sheila; I knew it would all be far too complicated for me to take in. Luckily, she didn't show any signs of telling me anything! Talking of luck, I was still wondering why she thought she'd need any. Perhaps I'd soon find out! Funnily enough, almost immediately a tall and impressive-looking crew member, who seemed to be in charge of the casino, said to Sheila,

"Oh, you've brought your lucky cat with you have you?! They both laughed. "Well, I hope so!" she responded.

She led me up and down the lines of machines. She seemed to be looking for one in particular. "Oh, yes," she muttered, "this is the one. This is my lucky machine from the last trip. Let's see if it's going to be kind to me again. I bet it won't be tonight though! I reckon, at least for a few days, it'll need to be fed a few dollars first." Fed? Surely these machines don't need feeding? She sat down on a stool in front of the machine and pushed one of her money notes into a slot in the machine's chest. Ah, that's how they eat! Immediately the machine made a fast "ding-ding-ding-ding-ding" noise and Sheila settled herself on her seat and put all her concentration into whatever the machine was doing next. It was making dinging and clinking noises and flashing lights and little pictures of fruit and bars were coming up on the front of its chest. I quickly lost interest. Each to his own, and this wasn't to mine!

After about half an hour I was feeling half deafened by all the noise around the place, with the countless machines dinging, pinging and, from time to time, sending out bursts of loud music. I got up and stretched. "Yes, okay Truffles," said Sheila, "I'm moving now. I'm not going to win anything tonight, but at least I've got my stake back and can use that to play tomorrow." She pressed a button on the machine and a slip of paper came out of its chest slot. Steak? Funny-looking steak - all thin and white; nothing like the brown grilled bits of the stuff I'd eaten earlier! Things on here were getting weirder and weirder, I decided.

We made our way out of the casino and instead of taking the elevator we went up one lot of stairs and arrived at a very nice coffee and seating area - not the one we'd passed by in the big promenade yesterday. This looked more classy. "I always like this place. I wonder if they'll let you sit under my chair if I just have a quick drink here," said Sheila. "I can but ask! It's not a major eating area and there are only a few people in here at this time of night." We went up to the counter, she explained about me to the person in charge, and we got permission! She sat down and I tucked myself away behind her legs. A tall glass of her frothy favourite was put in front of her and it had a rather strange extra aroma coming from it. I sniffed. Yuk! "Amoretto," she said. "You wouldn't like it, but I love an Amoretto coffee as my nightcap!" You can keep it, I thought, and I retired back behind her legs again. I dozed ... listening with half an ear to the odd comments coming from people passing by like: "Is that a real cat", "I know I've had a bit to drink but I've never seen cats before, only flying pigs," etc. I'd heard it all before!

Finally we left the coffee place and caught the elevator back to our deck. Once 'home' again, Sheila hung a notice outside the stateroom door, locked it, took off all her finery and changed into her night attire whilst I paid a last visit to the litter box. "Well, we've had a nice day, haven't we Truffles?" she said. "Tomorrow is another sea day and then we will be arriving at Gibraltar, which is a place rather like England but with better weather! It'll be the only place where I'll take you off the ship, as I'm not sure that you'd like the hustle and bustle of France, Spain, Italy and Portugal. It would be a bit frightening for you, I think. But I know Gibraltar and it will be much more peaceful and you will be okay with it there." I didn't know what she was talking about - all these strange places - but I took her word for it. As I said earlier, as a considerate cat carer, she would never take me anywhere she felt I wouldn't feel safe to be in. "But when I go and visit the other places, don't worry," she continued, "as I won't be leaving you alone all day. I'll only get off for the morning and will be back for a late lunch. What's the point of paying for lunch ashore, anyway, when you can have it on the ship for free?" With that, we both retired to our respective beds. I relived the events of the day in my mind before I dropped off to sleep, and I expect she did, too.

# Second sea day

We awoke to bright sunshine again, and as I went outside I could feel the much hotter sun on my fur. Yes, we did seem to be getting into warmer climes. What a treat! We don't seem to have had any really hot weather in Cornwall for the past two or three summers, except for the odd couple of days or so here and there. Certainly Sheila hasn't sat out in the garden as much as she did in previous years. I heard a knock at the door and a voice saying, "Room service," and the smiley food steward came staggering in with a large tray on which there were several plates and bowls. "Balcony, madam?" he said. "Yes, please," said Sheila.

After he'd gone, she said, "Come on, Truffles, breakfast time. I thought I'd have it here with you today. Wait until I've had my starter and then you can have yours." She helped herself to some of that sickly fruit and y... yo... yog... creamy stuff she likes. I waited impatiently for her to uncover the larger plates, as I could smell the tempting aroma of bacon, sausages and other good things. Everything comes to he who waits ... eventually ... and I was rewarded for my patience with a good helping of chopped bacon, sausage and egg, which she decanted into my bowl. "Don't expect this every breakfast time," she said. "It's just a one-off!" I was too busy gobbling it up to listen. When we'd finished, she sat there sipping her frothy drink - how many gallons of the stuff must she have drunk in her life? I wondered. Enough to sink the ship, I should think! We must have sat there for nearly an hour before another knock at the stateroom door heralded Eduardo's morning visit. "Oh, Eduardo, we'll be off in few minutes," she said, "sorry!" "It's quite all right, madam," he replied, "I'll come back later." Bother, I thought, I won't be here when he comes back, so I'll miss my extra morning treat! Still, I couldn't grumble, could I? Not after that rather splendid bacon breakfast!

After checking that my litter box was cleaned and empty and the stateroom tidy, Sheila gave me a quick brush, clipped on my nautical collar and lead and off we went. "I'm going to meet up with those people I met yesterday," she said, "to have a game of croquet, and you can have a nice nap on the grass up there in the sun." Good, I thought, nothing would suit me better! Up we went in the elevator again and I peered out through the glass, still wondering how living trees could be suspended in mid-air. I was beginning to think this was a magic ship! The unseen lady announced that we were on Deck 15 and out we got and walked towards the grassy area. When seeing it for the first time yesterday, I hadn't realised just how large it was. Several people were playing games on it, and others were sitting on it with little baskets by their sides containing various cheeses (I love cheese!) and bottles of those red and white liquids you love to drink. It was a peaceful scene, full of happy people. No wonder cruises are so popular, I thought.

Comfy-looking wicker chairs were set out in a row alongside the grass and Sheila spotted Connie and Ron sitting there, with a spare chair next to them. They exchanged greetings and I was patted. We sat down, watching some other people who were playing the ball and hoop game. "They'll be finishing soon," said Ron, "so then it'll be our turn. They've challenged us all to a match later on, so we'll show them how it's done!" They all laughed. I had a few doubts myself, as I knew that Sheila hadn't played for over five years and she probably couldn't even remember the rules. I hoped she wouldn't let the side down, but

I wasn't holding my breath! They continued their small talk while I sat and gazed around, until it was their turn to play. Sheila hooked my lead to a chair leg and they all walked onto the grass and started to select their wooden mallets and coloured balls. I felt a bit miffed at being tied up. I felt she didn't trust me! Fair enough, I pulled a few strokes in my youth, but nowadays I'm a model of good behaviour - well, apart from the towel incidents! Maybe she did it because she thought I would rush off to climb the mountain again! I wouldn't have, though, because I felt peacefully lazy and content in the warmth here and sleep wasn't going to be far away! I took a few paces onto the lovely grass and lay down lux... luxu... luxuria... feeling quite at home on it.

I soon fell into a doze whilst keeping half an eye open to watch them. I could hear the pleasant clunking sound of wood against wood as the three of them played, and occasionally, when someone got the ball through the hoop, they would give a small cheer. At other times, when they had a near miss, I heard the odd 'blue' word that you humans use when you're frustrated or angry - words that well brought-up pussycats like myself would certainly not dream of saying! After about half an hour they finished and more people came on to play. Sheila released my lead and they stood chatting for a few more minutes before the other two went on their way and we went ours. "I'll be meeting them again after lunch, as we'll be playing the 'match' against those other people," said Sheila, "so I guess I'd better not eat too much!" Easier said than done, I thought.

Back in our little haven once more, all was pristine and tidy, with bedding and towels changed, fruit bowl replenished - Eduardo had done his work well as usual! We sat outside and Sheila ate some of the fruit - it would never have tempted me. All those different coloured round (apart from some that looked like curved yellow sausages), sweet-smelling, squashy things are not in the least bit attractive to we cats. Fishy or meaty-smelling objects are much more to our taste! I've never been able to understand why you humans like such funny sickly smells. Back at home in the little room, next to the big ki... kit... kitch... cooking room, where Sheila does her washing and I have my litter box and food bowls, whenever I use said box Sheila dives under the sink and brings out a horrible sickly-smelling can of stuff, which she sprays into the air to take away my perfectly natural and pleasant catty odour. I hate it, but she hates my home-grown smells just as badly. Well, as I've said before, there's no accounting for tastes is there?

Lunchtime had come around again, so Sheila went to get hers and left me in peace on the balcony with a few cat crunchies to savour. I looked out over the big C again - still there was nothing except blue, blue and more blue as far as the eye could see! A bit boring, I thought, so I returned to the sunny corner again. Sleep mode set, I was away!

Sheila returned briefly, saying that she was off up to the grass again to play the match and when she got back she would take me to see one more sight I wouldn't forget in a hurry! I wondered for a moment what this ship would come up with next to astound me, before I fell asleep again.

Well, yes, I was astounded, and more than a little scared, as it turned out! When Sheila got back we went out and back up to the highest deck once more. It was heaving with people lying out in the sun or dipping themselves into the water pools. We rounded a corner and I heard a kind of roaring, splashing sound. I hung back. "Yes, I don't think you will really like this much, Truffles," she said, "but don't worry, nothing will hurt you. I just wanted to show you; it's so amazing to see this on a ship! We'll just have a quick look. We won't go too close, because I don't want to get splashed anyway." I was starting to get rather alarmed now. No way did I want to be splashed by some of the dreaded water! I could see a crowd of people all watching a large square water pool where the water was pouring down it in huge waves that were moving very fast. There were a couple of people on it standing up (or trying to!) on small wood planks and attempting to travel from one end of the pool to the other. The noise of the water spurting was horrendous. If I hadn't been tabby in colour I would have definitely paled! Oh dear, I wasn't keen on this. I applied my brakes and hid behind Sheila's leg. "We won't go any nearer," she said, "but I just want to watch for a few minutes. There are some seats up there, where we could sit for a while." However, on looking down at me trying not to quiver with fear and show myself up, she changed her mind, saying, "Oh dear, I didn't realise it would be quite so frightening. I'm sorry. Don't worry, we're going." She picked me up and cuddled me. I immediately felt safer.

Sheila set off fairly fast in another direction and I kept up with her without a backward glance. Soon we came to an area where several man passengers were running to and fro, kicking a ball about, and next to them some more were throwing a smaller red one at one poor man who was trying to fend it off with a kind of wood plank. Passing more lines of sun chairs with people lying on them, we came to a place that looked like lots of small green areas, each connected by paths. Each green patch had a hole in it and people were trying to push small white balls into the holes using long sticks. It seemed good fun, and I think I would have enjoyed joining them and patting the balls into the holes, though I wouldn't have needed a stick to do it – there's nothing as good as a front paw! I glanced up at Sheila - maybe we could have a go?

"Perhaps another time," she said. We carried on past an area covered with black and white squares where a couple were pushing what looked like small dinner plates, again with long sticks. What's with the sticks? I wondered. Can't they do it with their paws? That would be much more fun. Further on, a group of people were throwing thick circles of rope at a short pole, trying to l... la... lass... get them over the top of the pole. None of them managed it, I noticed! Lastly we came to a table where two young man passengers were furiously patting a small white ball to and fro, not with sticks this time but with round things they held tight in their paws. That was quite exciting to watch, I thought, and I got myself ready to chase and catch the ball if they dropped it. Unfortunately they didn't - pity!

So after our tour of the sports deck, very soon we were back at the elevator bank again. By this time I had managed to pull myself together, following the scary moments by the rushing water pool. I didn't want people to think I was a wimp. It is important for my ego (and I am told I have a big one since becoming a literary cat!) that in public I appear to be cool, calm and collected and certainly superior! Surprisingly, this time Sheila avoided going into an elevator and she walked me down a few sets of stairs before arriving at a room that was filled from floor to ceiling with books, rows and rows of them. I wonder if mine are here? I thought. As if reading my thoughts, Sheila said, "I'm just going to pick out a book to read. I should have brought some of yours with me - I could have put them out here for other people to read." She laughed. "More importantly," she went on, "they might have recommended them to their friends, who might go out and buy them!" Good idea, I thought.

At the next level down we stopped by an equally large room where there were lots of people sitting down at tables playing more games - indoor games this time, with cards or boards, and they were shaking little spotty square white cubes out of small containers shaped like drinking vessels, but not made of glass (about the only things on this ship that *weren't* made of glass!) Sheila stopped and watched for a while and then walked nearer to a table where a couple were playing a game using little bricks they had made into a wall and from which they were removing single bricks and - so it appeared to me - trying to make sets of three. The little bricks had pretty pictures on them. I remembered Sheila had a game like this - I was sure it had a foreign-sounding name, but I couldn't for the life of me remember it. As she was watching, the man looked up. "Do you like mah-jong?" he asked. "Oh, yes," replied Sheila. "My father lived in China many years ago and he brought home a beautiful antique set and we used to play it a lot, but I don't nowadays, I'm afraid. I play it on my computer instead, though it's not really a 'proper' game, just making up pairs really!" The man, who was rather flamboyant looking, sporting a handlebar moustache (for the uninitiated of you, a moustache means fur on your face!) said his name was David and he introduced Sheila to his wife, Irene. I took to them immediately - they both seemed very pleasant. Of course, they made the usual comments about my presence on board and Irene leant down and patted me. I purred at her, which made her smile. They chatted for a little while and agreed to meet up for a drink one evening, and then once more we were on our way.

Back at the stateroom, Sheila let me out onto the balcony and then disappeared, saying she was going to browse round the shops on board again before returning in time for the afternoon canapé delivery. I hoped she wouldn't return with another handbag! I just had time to fit in a nice little nap before she returned carrying a bag (not a handbag, a paper bag), which she opened to reveal a teddy bear attired in a cream vest bearing the ship's name in gold. "Cute, isn't he?" she said, sitting the bear down on a shelf next to a small bear called Curry Bear, who has been with her on every cruise she'd taken. He must have sailed thousands and thousands of miles all around the world. Sheila always says he is her good luck travelling bear and she'd certainly never go on a ship without him. Apparently, he came to her in quite an unexpected way. Some years ago she and her late partner, Peter, had parked their motor machine outside a very large well-known store that sold electrical stuff. When they came out, stuck behind those things on the front of the motor machine that push raindrops away was this little bear, who was wearing a sash over his chest with his name on it - like lady human beauty queens wear! Sheila fell in love with him right away and he's been with her ever since. Aaah!

How time flies when you're enjoying yourself, as they say. It was nearly canapé time again for her and afternoon nap time for me. We sat out in the sun, blinking in its brightness. Sheila generally wears those round glass things that hang on her ears and cover the front of her eyes, and she now replaced these with some black ones. How can she see anything now? I wondered. Very soon the smiley food steward arrived with her treats and, sitting with the remainder of the bottle of bubbly at her side, she sighed again. "This is the life!" It seemed to be her favourite saying since she'd been on board! Mind you, I felt I could understand now why she did like 'the life' so much - it was a million miles away from our quiet rural life together nowadays in Cornwall. No wonder she tells friends that she can't last more than six months of not being on board a ship before getting withdrawal symptoms! She knows that in my previous books I have made my catty observations on my own experiences of living in, and to a certain extent adapting to, a human environment. I was pleased that she had now thought to give me an insight into *her* 'other' life on a cruise ship. Now I understood it all much more and - I suppose - I should be more tolerant of her sticking me in the cat camp for the few weeks she is away each year. Over the years and at all other times she does faithfully cater to my every whim and need, I told myself, so she really does deserve her trips away. Oh dear, am I sounding a bit maudlin now? Sorry about droning on, but you get my drift, don't you?

We spent the next hour or so lapping up the sunshine and all was peaceful, with just the faint sound of music drifting over from some other part of the ship. I got up and wandered towards the edge to look at the C. Well, well, I thought, I can see something else right at the far-distant edge of the C! Green-topped grey/brownish hills were rising up out of it. I stood up, my paws resting on the glass wall, to see more. How exciting - it must be land! Hurray! Hurray!

The evening was not a 'formal night', so Sheila didn't take quite so long to get ready, though to my mind she still spent far too long fussing about her head fur. Perhaps she was hoping it would look as immaculate as mine always does - well, no chance dear! She had ordered in my dinner and I eagerly waited to see what would turn up. I wondered if it would exceed my expectations - and I have to say it did! It was a plate of delicious braised pork medallions. I never get the chance to eat much pork, because Sheila has always said that too much of it isn't good for cats. Too much? I've never had *much* of it, let alone *too* much of it! She chopped it up and I was almost drooling as she was doing it (but not quite, because to drool is bad manners and I, of course, have purrfect manners!) I gobbled down the pork while she put the last finishing touches to her outfit and sprayed that sickly smelling stuff on her neck. She waved me goodbye and went out, so I sat and had a lick-over, still savouring the delicious taste of the pork. Then I nipped up onto my cushion on the sofa for a doze and to digest my dinner. Even though I was now pleasantly full, I still wondered if Eduardo would bring me a treat when he came in later - I reckoned I could just about squeeze it in!

Eduardo arrived, so I got up and stretched before walking over to him and rubbing against his ankle. "'Ello, Trufools," he said, patting my head. "What 'av I got for you, eh?" He reached into his pocket and produced a little parcel, which he unwrapped to reveal several little white rings that smelt fishy! What on earth ...? I thought. "You'll like these, Trufools," he said, smiling as I looked up at him. "Squeeds!" Tentatively I took a bite and, yes, although they looked peculiar they were quite nice - not perhaps the best things I've ever eaten, but there again you don't know anything unless you try it! I'd thought that I would be tasting some new things on this ship, so I was glad to have the chance to try these fish rings. But I wouldn't be too disappointed if Eduardo didn't bring them again! I burped and returned to the sofa. He carried on with his duties and transformed a towel into something I didn't recognise in the least. "Sea lion," he said, as he gave me a goodbye pat. Blimey, I thought, I hope there aren't any lions out there swimming in the C! I wouldn't like to meet one of them out there - another reason to make sure I never fell overboard!

I was awakened some time later, when Sheila returned from her evening dinner. "Hello, Truffles," she said. "Well, that was another smashing meal and afterwards I went to a trivia quiz, which was fun. I met a nice couple there from Scotland called

June and Bobby. We made up a team together with another couple called Val and Ken, and as they came from Essex and I'm from Cornwall, we called ourselves 'The Triangles'. I blinked. How did she arrive at that? "Cornwall, Scotland and Essex make a sort of geographical triangle," she explained. "Never mind, Truffles, I know you don't know what geography is or what the hell I'm talking about anyway! We did okay - we didn't win, but we were in the top five. I think we might go to some more trivia sessions when they come up. One question stumped everybody. I bet you'd know, if only you could speak. The question was: what creature in the world has the longest tail? People suggested lemur, crocodile, blue whale and all sorts." What's an 'all sorts'? I wondered. "Anyway," she continued, "the answer was a giraffe! Nobody could believe it, but the question master said it had definitely been verified!" She shook her head in disbelief. "Right, come on, we'll pop into the casino and then have a night-time coffee again on the way back."

At the casino I resigned myself to a half-hour or so of the cac... caco... cacoph... bloody racket from all the hundreds of money-eating machines. I curled up underneath Sheila's chair whilst she sat repeatedly pressing the buttons on her favourite machine, trying to persuade it to cough up! Eventually she gave a squeak of excitement that made me jump, and the machine made an even more horrendous noise! "Oooh, Truffles, I'm fifty dollars up! Great! I'll stop now while I'm winning!" Sheila pulled out the little white slip of paper, with a big grin on her face. I wondered why, now that she was on a winning streak, she had stopped. If it were me in her paw covers, I would have carried on - but then I dare say I have more guts than she does!

We wended our way back up to the coffee place upstairs, getting the usual comments en route from people, such as: "Did the cat bring you luck" or "Is that a cat I can see, or have I had too much to drink?" Sheila sat down at the only empty table and ordered her Amoretto coffee. I lay down underneath her chair and observed. While she was waiting for the coffee, one of the ship's hossifers came up and asked if he could join her as the rest of the room was so full. "Of course!" she replied. He was rather handsome. I bet she's quite pleased that all the other tables are taken, I thought! I listened as they made the usual polite conversation, and then they started exchanging nautical stories.

Sheila had once lived in a coastal village in Cornwall where they did a lot of fishing. She told the hossifer about a rather eccentric man of the cloth, who would take services when a human's spirit had gone up to the sky to live but they had asked that their body be - for some reason I could never understand - buried under the water. Personally, I couldn't think of anything worse - I never want MY body to be put in any horrid water when I eventually go and join my old pussy pals in that big cat basket in the sky! I'll settle for being buried in the ground in a biscuit tin! I've heard these stories before many times and the people she's told them to have always found them quite amusing. Not that death is in the least a funny subject, but there again, there's often a bit of humour to be found in anything, even the saddest things. I thought you might like to hear some of these stories, which are all true - so here we go!

A person high up in the navy had passed on and it was decided that his body would be buried at sea in a designated area off the coast of Plymouth. The vicar was friendly with the skipper of a local fishing boat, and on several occasions in the past the boat had been used for such ceremonies. On the evening before the funeral the skipper of the fishing boat got the crew to give it a good clean and they rigged up an old door on which they intended to place the weighted-down body bag and then slide it down off the door and overboard at the appropriate moment. The next day dawned and the sad little group arrived on the boat - all the men in full naval uniform, complete with ceremonial swords, and all the ladies in their best hats. It was quite an upper-class turnout. The vicar proceeded with the service, and at the point where he said, "We commit his body to the sea," two of the crew members were supposed to raise the door up at a slight angle so that the body slid off. Higher and higher they raised the door, but nothing happened - the body in its weighted bag refused to slide off. Eventually the door was literally vertical and they were shaking it, and still they couldn't budge the body despite all their efforts. The door was lowered and they then realised what had happened. The night before, the skipper had decided to smarten up the door by giving it a coat of varnish. You've guessed it! It was still sticky and in the morning when the heavy body bag was placed onto it, well, it stuck fast! Oh dear, what a disaster! The poor widow was in floods of tears! Eventually they managed to prise the bag off and then the service went ahead. Afterwards the vicar told the two crew members that they had let him down badly, but really it was just an unfortunate accident and they'd had no way of knowing that the skipper had varnished the door after they'd left the boat the previous evening - neither had he realised that by the morning the varnish wouldn't have dried!

Another couple of disasters happened on cruise ships. Because cruise ships carry so very many people, they have to be prepared in case passengers become ill or even die, which does happen from time to time. A lady had cruised many times and, although she had died on land, she apparently had always said she would like to be buried at sea. So a little ceremony was arranged on a cruise ship for her relatives, and it had been planned for dawn, before most passengers had got up. The lady was small in stature and did not weigh very much. So the chief engineer of the ship said that they would have to weight the body bag down with some heavy bits of scrap iron from the engine room area. Accordingly, the bag was loaded with old heavy metal parts. The captain took the service, which went well, and the lady was released, as she had wished, over the side of the ship. Unfortunately, as the body bag fell downwards all the heavy stuff shot to the leading end, and so instead of landing on the sea in a horizontal position and then gradually falling to the seabed in a restful pose, the lady ended up going into the sea vertically, feet downwards, and planted herself in the seabed in that position! Afterwards, whenever the ship sailed over that particular part of the Red Sea, the captain always remembered the lady who would be standing forever upright on the seabed!

On another cruise ship a similar dawn ceremony was arranged. This particular ship had an antique brass gun turret that had been adapted to 'launch' bodies over the side. About half an hour or so before the ceremony, the captain came by to ensure that all was in order. It was. However, one of the crew members (who had been giving the brass a final polish), perhaps in awe of the captain watching him, inadvertently pressed the launching lever and - whoosh! - over the side the body bag went, right down to the bottom of the sea! There was no way that the bag could be retrieved, so everyone had to think quickly! In the end, when the relatives arrived for the service, all looked in perfect order. The ceremony went well and the relatives happily watched their loved one going to the final resting place he had requested only it wasn't their loved one that they were watching. They were bidding farewell to a body bag full of potatoes! Still, the man did end up in more or less the right place - just a few miles behind!

One last true story! This time it took place on a submarine. A retired submariner had died and had requested that his ashes were scattered at sea from the submarine on which he had served. The day arrived and the submarine sailed on the surface of the water to the area where the ashes were to be scattered. When it arrived at the spot, the vicar, carrying the urn and followed by the relatives, began to walk along the top of the deck to the bow, where he intended to carry out the service. As he was making his way there, he thought he'd better just check that the ashes inside the urn were okay and that he would be able to get the lid off smoothly at the appropriate time. He unscrewed the lid just as he was walking right by the submarine's air intake valves, and immediately all the ash was sucked out of the urn and disappeared into the valves! Some wag said, "Well, he'd always wanted to work in the engine room!"

The storytelling and their conversation ended, Sheila and the hossifer bade each other goodnight and he asked her if she was going to the Senior Hossifers' Cocktail Party the following week. She said she had already received an invitation so she would be there. What were these cocktail things everyone seemed to like so much? If they were made out of the rear ends of chickens, I would rather fancy one myself!

We went back to the stateroom and carried out our bedtime routines. "We'll have a walk into Gibraltar tomorrow morning, Truffles," said Sheila. We slept.

# Going ashore

We awoke bright and early and it was another beautiful day. I went out onto the balcony for my morning ablutions and then went to look through the glass wall. I was faced with a sight I had certainly never seen before! We were parked by the side of a dock similar to Southampton's, where many people bustled about and there were long gangways going down from the ship to the ground. Beyond that was a very big building, with many others dotted around the area. I could see another big cruise ship parked further down the dock - but not as gi... gig... gigan... big as our ship, I was pleased to note! And it was not nearly so smart. As readers of my diaries will know, I like to feel I am superior in everything I do, and being on the biggest and best ship in sight definitely made me feel superior! Further down the dock I could see lots of other smaller ships, but they weren't like our beautiful floating town; they were full of great big boxes and heavy-looking stuff and seemed very dirty, whilst our ship was gleaming white. I could see some of our crew members holding long sticks with what looked like bunches of twigs on the top and dipping them into cans of white stuff (milk perhaps?) and then wiping this white stuff over bits of the side of the ship where maybe there had been some mark. There was no doubt that this ship was pristine (yes, another posh word I have in my vocabulary!) inside and out at all times. Talking of the word 'posh', with the service and attention to detail all round, the passengers were made to feel like real celebrities on this ship. Mind you, I *am* a real celebrity!

Beyond the docks I could see a road leading to many more buildings, and behind them there were rows of houses like you live in back home. I wondered if the people here looked after cats, too! Further on I could see in the distance the green tops of trees and hills, and towering over everything in sight was a huge rock. It all looked very exciting and I couldn't wait to explore. Other than our back garden, the road outside our house and the various neighbours' gardens, I have to admit that I have never had the opportunity to look around anywhere else. So this was going to be the experience of a lifetime and I was jolly well going to make the most of it!

I turned to go back inside, and as I reached the patio door I nearly had kittens! Suddenly a shadow blotted out the sun. An extremely large bird, much bigger than me and mostly black with a bit of white on its tummy and an evil-looking beak - definitely by far the biggest and ugliest bird I've ever seen close up - landed on the rail on top of the outer glass wall! I gulped, but my natural reactions kicked in and I took a hefty sideways swipe at it. Sadly, I missed and slithered to a halt at the foot of the wall in a heap! Oh, the shame of it! The bird flapped off, giving me a mocking glance over its shoulder, and joined another one that was perched on a roof opposite. I looked over at them, growling under my breath. How dare they make a fool of me! I've seen the odd seagull before when they've come into our garden, scavenging for the food that Sheila puts out for the little birds. (Well, she likes them to keep their strength up so they can get away from me and the cats next door!) These two, though, were not just ordinary-sized seagulls. They were seriously big and pretty menacing. I'd never seen birds quite like them before - oh, perhaps they were the mysterious birds with the cock tails? My legs were a bit wobbly, but I pulled myself together and casually wandered into the stateroom. It would never do for Sheila to see me discomposed by a bird!

A mortifying moment!

"We'll have breakfast early," she said, "and then we'll go ashore." She decanted some turkey chunks topped with crispy sprinkles into my dish and disappeared to get her own breakfast. I ate quite slowly, still seething over the birds. Afterwards I went outside again, but they had gone. Good riddance, I thought, and don't come and pay us a visit again!

Sheila returned, gathered together her money, ship's card and my passport papers and stuffed them into her bag. She got out another one of my collars - this time a white one with a natty little silvery anchor hanging from the front with my name on it, attached the lead and we set off. At the elevators we had to wait a few minutes because everybody else seemed to have the same idea as us. Eventually one arrived and we all piled in - what a squash it was, too. I was surrounded by about twelve sets of large paws and it was a job not to get stepped on. The unseen voice announced that we were at Deck One and, relieved, we got out. Then there was another bit of a hold-up behind a long line of passengers who were heading slowly towards a square of sunlight ahead. When we eventually reached the sunlight there were two crew members waiting, smiling (as they always do) and wishing us a pleasant day ashore. Sheila put her card into the machine that pinged and then picked me up and showed the crew member my papers as well. They smiled and one, in a peculiar accent, said, "Cat!" Gosh, he's observant, I thought sarcastically! (I was still in a minor huff following the bird incident). We followed the other people and walked outside into the bright sunshine. Sheila hung her black shades in front of her eyes and we walked down a steep, narrow gangplank that took us down to the dockside. Wow, I'm on solid ground again, I thought. Not that I'd felt any particular movement on the ship during the entire journey so far, but it was nice to be off all that dreaded water for a while!

As we reached the dock I could see several of the crew members all dressed up as furry animals and there were two more that held picture-making gadgets in their paws. We stopped, Sheila picked me up and we posed (with me giving my best Cheshire cat grin) for a picture, standing beside one of these furry creatures. I looked at her and she laughed and said, "They're dressed up like the apes. Apes are like monkeys, Truffles, and they live at the top of the rock here. I've seen them before, but perhaps we'll just have a quick trip up there so you can see them, too." I was totally confused. Apes? Monkeys? I did know what a monkey was like, as I'd found out from the moving-picture machine at home. I still don't know why she calls ME a monkey sometimes, though! So if these apes look a bit like monkeys, then why aren't they called monkeys? Your human way of naming things certainly bewilders me at times!

We continued walking along the dock with a stream of other passengers and then Sheila led me in the direction of the large building I had seen from the balcony earlier. It was nice and cool inside and we passed through a large area with a cold floor made of shiny stone and some shops on either side of it. I saw that there were some of those machines that we had passed through at Southampton, with several bored-looking male humans standing beside them. They were dressed in matching outfits, but not nautical like the crew wear on the ship - theirs were a drab brown sort of colour and they wore dark green small hats with shiny silver badges. I didn't like the look of them - they looked a bit fierce! As we approached them, one stopped Sheila and, looking down at me, said, "What is that?" Oh no, I thought, I'm not being called a 'that' again, am I? I glared up at him, at the same time easing myself closer to Sheila's leg! But she showed him my papers and he waved us on through. When I turned around he was staring at us and scratching his head and his pals were all laughing! Why IS it that so many people laugh on seeing me on this holiday? Nobody laughs at me at home!

Out we came into the hot sunshine again. It was lovely. "Come on," said Sheila, "there's a coach going to the rock and we'll get on it and nip up there to see the apes," I wasn't sure what a coach was, but it turned out to be a very long motor machine with lots of windows and seats. She carried me onto it and we sat at the back. I looked out of one of the windows and marvelled at the scenery that we were passing. We seemed to be climbing and I realised that we were going up to the big rock that do... domi... domin... looked over the whole of this Gibraltar place. Soon the coach stopped and we got out. We walked a bit and Sheila spent some time looking at the view around us. There were lots of trees and bushes and very brightly coloured flowers that were nothing like the ones we have in Cornwall. There were also lots of tasty-looking little birds flying about tantalisingly. They looked different from the ones at home, too. Interesting. We were now very high up and I could see our big ship in the distance at the bottom, but from here it looked like a very little ship. We walked a bit further and came to a giant picture of a big monkey by the side of a doorway, which seemed to be cut right through a piece of the rock. Sheila fumbled in her bag and passed some of her money notes to the elderly lady human sitting by the door, and in return she was given a bag of treats! "No, it's not for you, Truffles," she said, guessing my thoughts. "This is for the apes. It's macaroni - they love it." Weird, I thought. It wasn't even cooked, so it was rock (excuse the pun!) hard. I had a taste of macaroni cheese once – well, I like cheese, but I thought the macaroni was a bit slimy, rather like a slug!

We passed through the door and I saw a lot of other people, not all from our ship, who were watching quite a large group of the famous apes! They (the apes, not the humans) were gambolling about and climbing up and jumping down from the surrounding low walls. They were also trying to grab people's picture-making machines and handbags. One man had his hat stolen! I noticed that Sheila was hanging on tightly to her own handbag! I don't know why she was worried - she's got so many that I'm sure she wouldn't miss one! Going back to the apes, I was totally shocked! I had expected them to be brown-furred, large and overpowering, and that I would be frightened, but they were not much larger than me - well, yes they were, but I reckoned they were only about the size of a Labrador dog, though not the same shape. They were more like miniature humans in shape, as far as I could see, and their fur was a pale grey colour. I was fascinated by them. Sheila threw some of the macaroni pieces to the one that was nearest to us. He grabbed the pieces in his front paws and put them in his mouth. I was bemused. How did he pick up things in his paws? Cats can't do that - we can push and pat things about, but we can't pick things up like that. I felt a twinge of jealousy. I've always thought we cats are the smartest and most cleverest animals on earth, and yet here in some foreign country was an ape/monkey doing something that I could only dream about! What, with the encounter with the big black bird and now this, I was beginning to get an inferiority complex! It was certainly becoming a day I wouldn't forget in a hurry. We watched the antics of the apes for a while, keeping our distance. I felt that Sheila didn't want us to make contact, as whenever an ape looked as if it was going to get too close she drew me back. "You mustn't get too near, Truffles," she said. "Despite you having those injections, I don't want you to touch any other animal whilst we're away from England. Come on, we're going now." So we left the top of the rock and got into another long motor machine. We soon arrived back near to the dock area. I thought we were going back to the ship, but Sheila turned the other way and we started to walk towards the crowd of buildings and houses I had seen from the ship.

You can keep your macaroni, mate!

It felt very strange to be walking, attached on the lead to Sheila, along a busy road because, as I said earlier, I had never been out before on even the quiet road where we live! I have only sat in our garden and watched people, sometimes accompanied by their dogs, walk by. So now I would have a chance to put myself in the place of a dog (heaven forbid!) and see for myself how it felt. The dogs I'd seen didn't seem to mind the motor machines roaring past them on the road, but here I must say it was quite alarming, because the motor machines that passed us were very large and very noisy. So I must admit that I did feel glad to be secured to Sheila, as I don't think I could have coped with it all on my own - I would probably have been a complete wimp and rushed and hidden behind the first wall I came across!

It was still very hot, so Sheila's pace was slow, which suited me as it gave me more of a chance to drink in my surroundings. So strange and different from Cornwall! Suddenly I noticed a large ginger and white tomcat sitting on a stone seat watching me. Sheila's grip tightened on my lead. As we reached the seat the cat got up and spat in the most rude manner at me! Well, that wasn't very welcoming, I thought. Mind you, if any cat I don't recognise dares to come into our garden at home I also give it a load of abuse, but I don't stoop so low as to spit! This cat obviously hadn't been brought up well as I had. In cat lingo I gave it a piece of my mind and was rewarded with a torrent of abuse, but in a strong accent that I didn't recognise! Sheila tugged at the lead and as we went on by I had the last word and let rip in my Cornish accent, which left the other cat speechless!

We sauntered on. It grew even hotter. As we approached an even bigger road with lots more motor machines roaring to and fro, I spotted a second cat lying stretched out on top of another seat. This time it was a pale grey and white and very pretty (I grudgingly have to admit) young female cat. She was quite a different kettle of fish from the other b-----d. She got down from the seat and said (in cat), "Hello to you, stranger! My name is Misty. Welcome to beautiful Gibraltar. Where have you come from? I've never seen you before." I told her that I was from Cornwall and was having a cruise on the big ship and she was most impressed. She had never been on a ship. I didn't tell her it was my first time - I sort of let her get the impression I was a seasoned traveller! We made small talk for a few minutes while Sheila sat on the seat, and then we said our goodbyes. Sheila picked me up and we crossed over the big road and carried on towards the town. Thankfully, the road now became much quieter and there were no motor machines on it - just lots and lots of humans.

Very soon we stopped in a large square surrounded by many small, brightly decorated shops, including several of the frothy coffee places that Sheila likes. She led me towards one of them and we sat down outside it under a leafy tree. That's nice, I thought - much as I like sitting in the sun, it really was very hot here. I wished my fur catsuit had a zip in it that I could loosen! Out came a nice-looking young man human, who smiled and asked what Sheila wanted. She returned his smile, ordered a large frothy coffee drink and also asked if he could bring a saucer of water for me. He smiled even more broadly. "Certainly," he said. "I've never seen a tourist with a cat before!" "Well, there's always a first time," said Sheila. We sipped our drinks and both lazily looked around the big square. I was enjoying the sight of the humans in all shapes and colours who were wandering about, some speaking in languages that were totally foreign to me. Several came up and patted me and spoke to Sheila. We were certainly attracting attention! Well, after my rather humiliating experience earlier with the monster bird, it was all good for my ego! After half an hour Sheila got up and tugged on my lead and off we went again.

In front of us was a long and, to me, never-ending road crammed on each side with shops selling everything under the sun, but most of them were full of all those sparkly ornaments that Sheila likes to decorate her neck and paws with. She must have stopped outside every one of them whilst she peered through the windows at the dazzling displays. It soon got boring for me. I was looking out for a pet shop, but I didn't see one. They obviously didn't cater much for cats here. I should have asked Misty if there was one around. I'd noticed she was wearing a designer pink collar, which must have come from somewhere! Eventually we went into one of the sparkly shops and, after a brief consultation with the owner, Sheila picked out a bright pink sparkly thing to hang round her neck, with a matching smaller one for around her paw. She seemed very pleased with them. Good for her, I thought, uncharitably, but what about something for me? As if she'd read my thoughts again, she told me that she knew of a pet shop upstairs in an arcade of shops and we would call in there on the way back. I brightened up!

We had by now walked right up to the end of the street of shops, Sheila going inside a few more and buying various odds and ends. Now I knew what she used this money stuff for - giving it away to shops and feeding the machines in the casino! Then we headed back down the other side again, meeting several people she recognised from the ship on the way, who all stopped to have a brief chat. One was a very smart lady called Margaret who, like Sheila, seemed to be a very keen shopper, as she was carrying about six or seven large paper bags in her paws. They chatted and arranged to meet up at some of the future ports of call to do some shopping together. "I won't have Truffles with me any more," Sheila explained. "I think Gibraltar will have been enough for her!" Margaret nodded in agreement. "She certainly wouldn't like the traffic in Florence or Rome." she said. They smiled at each other and we parted company, Margaret going in the direction of a big shop called M & S and us heading off to find the pet shop.

It didn't take long to reach the arcade and we climbed up some steep stairs to get to the upper floor - no elevators here! We got to the shop and went inside. The first thing I saw was a cage with about six tiny kittens in it. Sheila took me over to look at them and the kittens shrank back in alarm. "It's okay," I told them, "don't be frightened, I won't eat you!" They calmed down and mewed hesitantly at me, saying they didn't know where their mummy was. I remembered when I, too, was very small and alone and scared. I had been kept in a similar pen at an animal rescue centre until Sheila and Peter came and took me to their home. "Some nice human carers will very soon come along and give you good homes," I told the kittens. "Just hang on in there and all will turn out okay in the end." Sheila cooed over the kittens for a few minutes and then dragged me to the other side of the shop, where there were packets of cat treats, cat toys, collars and all sorts of stuff. She got out her money again and bought me a nice big bag of cheesy treats and a rather unusual collar that was in a kind of faux fur leopard-skin pattern. Pretty cool, I thought!

We continued on our way and I could see the outline of the ship in the distance. However, when we arrived back at the square again Sheila decided that it was a bit late to go back for lunch on the ship and in any case she was so hot that she wasn't really all that hungry. Me neither. So she picked out another of the coffee places that looked nice and took a seat outside, whilst I flopped down under the table in the shade. She ordered a large mug of her frothy favourite and a prawn roll. My ears pricked up at the word 'prawn', although I didn't know what she meant by a roll - the only roll I knew about was the one I often do on the grass, but surely she can't have meant that! Maybe the heat was making me confused. More than likely it was another mishmash of your human language, where one word means more than one thing, but I couldn't be bothered to tax my brain in the heat by trying to work it out!

As we sat there, waiting for the drink and the prawn roll, Sheila saw Margaret walking up. "Come and join us for a coffee. I've just ordered," she said. "Yes, I'm dying for a drink," panted Margaret, and she sat down at the table. No wonder she was sweating buckets, I thought. I noticed that since we had last seen her, her paper bag collection had grown to at least ten! A further coffee and roll ordered, we all sat peacefully. After begging for - and getting - a couple of prawns from each of them, I half closed my eyes and let the sound of their chatter lull me to sleep. All they seemed to be talking about was shopping, and it sounded as if Margaret virtually lived in the place called M & S whilst Sheila spent most of her time in another place called TKM. I wondered why they were talking in a kind of code! And what did the code letters stand for? I mused idly. M & S - perhaps the Mouse and Shrimp emporium? Well, that would be my favourite place to shop anyway! And TKM might be The Kipper Market. Well, I can dream, can't I?

Time went by and, refreshed and rested, we started on the journey back to the ship. It was still very hot, but they weren't walking fast and so, despite being lumbered by my close-fitting fur coat, I didn't get overheated. We passed the seat where I had chatted to Misty, but she wasn't there. Pity, I thought. Nearer the dock we came to where the ill-mannered white and ginger tom had been sitting, but he wasn't in sight either. Good, I thought! Finally we arrived at the big building behind which the ship lay waiting for us. We stood at the back of a long line of passengers and waited as they slowly shuffled forward, and I saw that the fierce-looking men in the drab outfits were making them walk through an archway and put all their belongings onto a moving platform, where they disappeared into a magic tunnel, similar to the one they'd had at Southampton. I sincerely hoped they'd not force me to go in the tunnel - they didn't look so cheery as the officials at Southampton; in fact, they looked quite nasty, particularly a fat and sweaty one who was glowering quite openly at us. I prepared myself for a confrontation. I think Sheila did, too, as she pulled me closer to her and held tightly to my passport and papers.

"Wait!" barked the official. "What's that? You can't bring that through!" Oh, here we go again, I sighed. Sheila gave her usual explanation and waved my passport at him. "You must wait here," he responded with a frown. "I'm going to check this." He waved Margaret on. "Shall I wait with you?" she said worriedly to Sheila, who replied that it was quite okay and she'd see her later. So Margaret gave me a comforting pat, whilst the official glared at her and told her to get a move on and hurry up. "Don't you dare talk to me like that," she snapped, returning his glare, "and don't you dare tell me what to do either! Nobody does that and certainly not a lump like you!" Cheers and clapping came from the people waiting behind us and the nasty official had the grace to look a bit sheepish. "Come over here, you," he said to Sheila. "I've never seen the likes of this before. A tourist with a cat, indeed!" "Well," responded Sheila bristling, "Nobody worried at

Southampton and nobody here stopped us when we came off the ship this morning." (Another cheer came from behind!) "Truffles' papers are all in order and here is her ship's ID card as well. She's a very important cat, specially invited on board, and that's why she's here!" "Oh, well," the man blustered, "I suppose it will have to be okay, but the cat must go through the X-ray arch so we can see there's nothing hidden in her collar." "Oh, for goodness' sake - we've nothing to hide!" said Sheila, and she dragged me through the archway. No unseen mice squeaked or pinged and we passed through with no problem. The official scowled at us, but said nothing more. His men behind him tittered. The passengers behind clapped. Sheila snatched up her stuff from the end of the magic tunnel. "He's certainly got a serious attitude problem," she said to Margaret, who was waiting on the other side. "Yes," agreed Margaret, "We didn't spend thousands on a cruise to be spoken to like that!" She's really on her high horse now, I thought. "Oh, well," said Sheila, "I suppose they've never seen a cat coming off a cruise ship before and they just didn't know how to handle it. That bloke didn't look very bright to me - more brawn than brain. Anyway, it won't happen again. This was just the reason I decided not to take Truffles off at any other port - imagine if we'd had this little scene with some bunch of over-excited Italian or Spanish officials!" They laughed together and the tension eased.

As we got to the side of the ship I saw a group of several comfy wicker sofas with some of the food stewards standing by them holding trays of cool drinks and also little wet towels so that people could wipe their hot faces. "How thoughtful they are on this ship," remarked Margaret as she and Sheila accepted a couple of glasses and sat down on one of the sofas. "Yes," said Sheila. "After all that palaver I certainly need a rub down with a damp flannel!" They giggled. "Still," she went on, "it wasn't the ship's fault and I don't reckon we would have been in any trouble with the port authority either, as Truffles is travelling with all the right papers. They're generally most polite here. I've been here loads of times and the officials are usually very friendly. I think that thickhead was just a proper bad-tempered old grump who'd got out of bed on the wrong side!" I didn't recognise the terms 'thickhead' or 'grump', but they sounded unflattering so must have described that horrible human purrfectly! We sat for few more minutes. I noticed that the passengers who were returning to the other cruise ship parked nearby did not have the luxury of chairs, drinks and cooling towels to meet them on arrival. Some were casting looks of envy at us. Yes, this is the life, I thought, feeling superior again! No wonder Sheila raves about this particular cruise line!

We climbed up the gangway, which seemed at a considerably steeper angle now. Once more we faced an inspection process. What a difference between our friendly crew officials and that man in the port, though! All smiles this time, with no glares. Sheila popped our cards into the machine and put her shopping onto the moving surface, where it passed smoothly through the magic tunnel. Margaret followed with her mound of bags and we all stepped through the archway without any incident and arrived back at the elevator meeting place. "See you this evening," said Sheila as we parted company with Margaret, and a short time later we were back at our stateroom again.

It was nice to be 'home' again after my exciting day ashore in a foreign country! I'd seen things I could never have imagined: the apes, the big rock, the long motor machine, plus all the hustle and bustle of the shops and coffee places where so many people co... con... conger... got together. I was definitely getting more of an insight into human life! I was also coming to understand more and more each day why so many of you love cruising!

I went out on the balcony and relieved myself in the litter box. "Phew," said Sheila, following me out, "I'd better deal with that quickly before the room service steward arrives!" Job done (excuse the pun again!) she sat down while I lay in my usual corner. She was just in time, as seconds later a knock heralded the arrival of today's canapés and she brought them outside. Also, another bottle of bubbly had appeared on the table, so she poured herself a glass from it. We sat peacefully nibbling at our treats (it was some tiny slithers of quails' eggs for me). Suddenly Sheila looked up and said, "Oh, Truffles, look at that giant bird sitting over there - you've never seen a bird like that!" "Wanna bet?" I muttered. It was, of course, the same murderous-looking bird I'd had the run-in with earlier. "Isn't he lovely?" she went on. "He's called a Frigate Bird. I've seen some before on another cruise, but never here - I think it could have been off South America somewhere." She stood up and went to the edge to get a closer look. Personally, I had no wish to see it any closer! "It's a pity he won't fly nearer," she said, "but he'll be frightened of getting too near to the ship." If only you knew, I thought! As she stood there, the neighbours came out onto their balcony and Sheila started chatting to them. "Do you see that bird over there?" she said, pointing. They looked and the man said how wonderful it was to see it and that it was such a pity we never got them in England. Thank God for that, I thought! "Maybe it's just as well," said Sheila. "If Truffles saw one she'd probably have kittens!" They all burst into laughter. "No need to keep going on about it," I grumbled under my breath. I was sick of hearing about that wretched bird!

After a while the ship made its loud barking noise and we

slowly started to move away from Gibraltar. The rock, the apes and the shops all disappeared from view and once more I could see nothing but the big blue C. I reclined and reflected on my exciting trip ashore. From what Sheila had said, I realised that I wouldn't be going ashore any more. But she must have had good reason, so I guessed that she was thinking of my welfare as usual. To be honest, today had been exciting for me but also somewhat overwhelming. It had certainly been a once in a lifetime experience that I wouldn't forget in a hurry!

I heard Sheila ordering my dinner and, wondering what it would be, I went inside. She was sitting on the sofa, watching the moving-picture machine. She had changed her outer coverings and I saw that she was wearing her new sparkly purchases. "I'm going out a bit earlier this evening, Truffles," she said. "I'm going to see the ice show." I wondered what an ice show was. She had explained to me what a 'show' was - something on this ship where people dressed up and entertained the passengers - but how could one be made of 'ice'? I couldn't get my head round it. I remembered seeing ice at home last winter. Awful stuff - I hated it. I had woken up one morning and found that the green grass was covered with a thick layer of white and this ice stuff was all over the patio and the path that ran round the edge of the house. Sheila had opened the back door to let me out but, on seeing that everything within sight was entirely white, I lost my nerve and stayed exactly where I was. She coaxed me out and told me to be brave and go and try it. So I took a tentative step. OMG! It was cold to the paws! Brrrr! I took a couple more small steps and it felt all slippery. I quickly jumped over the pathway onto the white grass! Mistake! I sunk into its covering of white nearly up to my shoulders. What on earth was all this? I remembered some years earlier seeing a very thin smattering of white one day on the grass, but it had disappeared by the evening. I turned around to see Sheila laughing at me (well, as you know, I don't like to be laughed at and I was surprised to see her, who should know better, doing it) and I gave her a filthy look. "Sorry, Truffles," she'd said, "but it's so funny seeing you in the snow!" (So that's what the white stuff was called!) It was okay for her - she has much longer legs than me. She wouldn't have sunk into this snow stuff up to her shoulders! There was no way I was going out to do my ablutions in the freezing cold, and that was that - she had another thing coming if she thought otherwise. I darted back inside and that was the last time I went outside the house for a couple of weeks, until the snow and ice had disappeared!

Remembering this, though, didn't explain to me how she could be going to an 'ice show' here on the ship. But don't go there, Truffles, I thought - it will all be beyond you! So I just sat and waited for my dinner to arrive with the smiley food steward, whose name, I had learnt, was Marcello.

Dinner arrived and whatever was under the silver dome smelt very good. "'Ow ees puzzy today?" smiled Marcello, as he placed the dish on the table. Sheila told him that we'd been ashore in Gibraltar and asked if he had managed to get some time off the ship, too. He said he had been too busy, but hoped to get off for a few hours when we reached some place called Florence. He patted me goodbye and left. I would have given him a purr, but my mouth was watering due to the tantalising smell of my dinner and I didn't want to disgrace myself by dribbling all over the carpet! Sheila took off the dome to reveal some lamb cutlets. I licked my lips. She chopped them up into small pieces and put them in my dish. "Mmmm," she said, "these look good. I might have lamb myself tonight!" But I'm getting the first taste, I thought, as I started to demolish my dinner. After a glance around to check that everything was neat and tidy as usual, Sheila left to go to the puzzling ice show and her lamb dinner.

Much later she returned. I was sound sleep in my bed in the corner. Eduardo had been in earlier and had seen to everything in his usual efficient way, turning down the bed and replacing the towels and fruit and even the flowers this time, but though they were just as brightly coloured the new flowers still didn't have any butterflies on them for me! He also left a natty bag on the bed for Sheila. Another bag, I thought, she'll be pleased. It was in nautical colours and had the ship's name on it. As I looked and sniffed at it, Eduardo had said, "Tote bag, Truffles. Pleeze don't scratch on it," Ah, good, I thought - at last somebody has been helpful enough to tell me exactly what something is without my having to puzzle about it for ages. Now I know Sheila can carry her totes in it! Sheila was pleased to see the tote bag and said it would be very handy when she went ashore. She buckled my new leopard-print collar around my neck, which fortunately fitted, and then said, "Come on, it's casino time, Truffles! I groaned and followed her.

I lay beside her in the casino, trying, without success, to nod off in the wretched noisy place, and from the sound of her occasional loud squeaks she was enjoying herself and her machine was being kind to her! Suddenly I felt her rising from her seat and turning around. She was greeted by the hossifer she'd had coffee with the previous evening. He was accompanied by another hossifer - a taller man in a very grand white two-piece set of outer coverings, with what looked to me like bits of gold rope stuck on top of his shoulders and also ringing the end of his sleeves. The first hossifer was similarly dressed but more low key, with not nearly so much gold. He introduced the tall man to Sheila as the Master of the ship. They shook paws and then the Master bent down and said to me, "Good evening Truffles, I've been told all about you. I do hope you are enjoying my ship. I am delighted to meet you. We have never had a cat on board before!" He stroked me and I pulled out all the stops and gave him my best Cheshire cat grin and a big purr. I realised that he must be a very important person. "This is the Captain, Truffles," said Sheila. "He is in charge of the entire ship, so you must be on your best behaviour whenever you see him!" They all laughed. After a few more minutes chatting, the hossifers moved on and Sheila sat back down again. "Well, you were honoured there, Truffles," she said. I preened myself - well, I thought so too, but there again, the Captain was lucky to meet me as well! After a bit more button pressing, the machine gave Sheila its little paper slip and we left the casino en route for the frothy coffee place and her late-night Amoretto coffee drink. I wondered if she was hoping that her hossifer might join her again, but he was nowhere to be seen - still with his big boss, I expect!

In bed that night I started to recall all that had happened that day, but before I got very far I had fallen fast asleep and didn't wake up again until the bright sun was streaming through the patio doors!

# Another sea day

After we awoke, we both went onto the balcony - me to the litter box and her to lean out over the glass wall and breathe in the fresh air. As I sat on the box, I mused - it was so different here from the air we got at home. Sounds silly, I know; after all, air is air wherever you are and the Cornish air is well known for being healthy and fresh itself. But here it was kind of different - the 'warming Mediterranean air', as I'd heard people describe it when I'd been listening in to their conversations. Whatever it was, we'd not had such warm air at home for months, so I was going to make the most of it!

After Sheila had finished her own ablutions, dressed herself and tidied up generally, she got me my breakfast, which today was creamed salmon pâté sprinkled with a few prawn crunchies. Nice! Then she went out for her own breakfast. I ate at a leisurely pace and then returned outside and lay down right by the glass wall overlooking the C. I marvelled at myself - who would have thought that only three days ago I would have been scared of going so close to the edge! I sat and watched the white froth that the ship made as it moved through the C. It was quite hy... hyp... hypn... fascinating and I was almost in a trance by the time Eduardo arrived. "'Ello, Trufools," he said, coming out and patting me on the head. "You are enjoying the big sun, yes?" Yes, I was. He stood alongside me for a moment and then shook his head, saying he must get on. I heard him carrying out the daily sheet changing and going over the carpet with the machine that I just hate. Sheila has one at home and it sounds like a colony of angry wasps fighting when she switches it on. She walks up and down the rooms with it, doing I don't know what - at the end of it all nothing looks any different to me! A simply pointless exercise, as far as I'm concerned. So why she and Eduardo are so keen on dragging these machines about beats me!

Later on, Sheila reappeared and she was carrying a bag. Oh dear, she's been down to the shops again, I thought, giving more of her money away! I don't know what she had bought this time, because she never showed me and just put the bag away in a cupboard. She got out my nautical collar and clipped on the lead. "Come on, we'll go up on deck and sit for a while," she said. "I might read my library book or people watch." We followed the usual route via the elevators and arrived at the deck with all the water pools and sun chairs on it, not the grassy deck above. It was heaving with people sunbathing, but Sheila was lucky and found a low chair to lie on. I sat half underneath it. A sickly smell wafted down to me. Yuk! Looking up, I could see that she was smearing some oily-looking stuff from a little bottle onto her face and arms. What's she doing that for? I wondered. I wouldn't like my fur to get all clogged up with oil. Still, it was nothing to do with me, so I settled down again and, thankfully, not very long afterwards the offensive smell soon di... dis... disp... went away. We sat there drowsing in the sunshine, with Sheila making the usual replies to comments from passers-by about seeing me on board. I began to get a little fed up with all the pats on the head from so many sweaty paws!

Suddenly a huge shadow blotted out the sun. Surely it wasn't that vile bird again? I sat up. Thank goodness it wasn't! The people next to us also sat up, the drone of their chattering dying away. A huge lady human - the biggest and fattest I'd ever seen - came waddling past us in the direction of the water pool. "Crikey," gasped Sheila, "that must be the woman Dianne at the table nicknamed Mrs Golightly!" She stared at Mrs Golightly in a bemused fashion. I drew back under the chair a bit more - I would have been crushed if this monster human had stepped on me. "Good God," said the man sitting by us, "she's at least three times the size of my mother-in-law, and that's saying something!" We all watched in awe as Mrs Golightly wobbled on towards the pool. She was almost wearing a brief two-piece outfit, like you humans wear for your unpleasant pastime of swimming, and that outfit certainly left little to the imagination! It hardly reached over all her lumps of fat. I remembered once seeing a picture of an enormous white person that looked as if it was made out of balloons, advertising those things that you put on the wheels of your motor machines. Well, to my mind she looked like that! Mrs Golightly seemed completely ob... obl... obliv... unaware of the stir she was causing. She didn't seem to notice the silence; she just kept lumbering on. Eventually she arrived at the water pool. There were only five or six young people in it, and when they caught sight of her they panicked and all jumped out of the pool, some crying and the others laughing hysterically. They rushed to their respective mothers.

Mrs Golightly, taking no notice of anybody whatsoever, plonked herself down on the edge of the pool and slithered into the water. Immediately, a great gush of water overflowed from the pool and the people sitting in the chairs close by moved back a bit smartish so they wouldn't get wet. She just sat there in the water as if nobody else was around. Well, I suppose she was happy. Certainly she was making most of the people watching happy, as I could hear lots of giggling. I noticed that quite a lot of people were pointing their little talking machines or picture-making machines in her direction - obviously recording her posterior for posterity!

Take cover! Mrs Golightly's about!

"Well," said Sheila, "there's me, who would never dare to go out in public nowadays with shorts on, what with my thighs (oh dear, her obsession with her thighs, I sighed - they've always looked okay to me!) and blimey, look at her, she doesn't care a hoot!" "I don't want to look at her," said the man next door. "It's making me feel ill. I think I'll go and get a pint!" And he got up and moved off. His wife smiled at Sheila. "At least after seeing her," she said, "he'll now appreciate what he's got." I looked about at the other people and, although some were thin and some were fat, none were anywhere near Mrs Golightly's size. People were dressed in all sorts of weird swimming costumes or sun-worshipping outfits - and not all of them flattering, I can tell you. But on holiday everyone just wants to relax and enjoy themselves and I expect that's why they wear all these funny outer coverings that they'd probably never dream of wearing back at home.

After a while, as Mrs Golightly did not appear to be about to move, interest died and the hum of chatter started up again. Nobody else got into the pool - well, there wouldn't have been enough room, would there? And I expect the children were too frightened. After about half an hour she dragged herself out of the pool, shook herself a bit, giving us all a sick-making display of wobbling flesh, and lumbered back the way she'd come. A collective sigh came from the other sun worshippers and things returned to normal, although I noticed that nobody else fancied going in the pool!

A little later Sheila had baked enough in the hot sun, so she said, "Come on, Truffles, let's go and see what's happening on the grass deck." That sounded good to me, so off we went. When we got up there we could see quite a lot of people playing games with balls and Sheila waved to Ron and Connie, who were playing the ball and mallet game with four other people. "How are you?" called Connie. "Come and join us this evening in the Martini Bar before dinner." "Great," said Sheila, "see you there at about 7.30." There were no empty seats nearby, so we walked round to the other side of the grassy space to find one. She sat down and I lay on the grass and had a pleasant roll! We spent the rest of the morning there. It was lovely.

My tummy was signalling that it must be nearly my lunch crunch time and Sheila must have thought so, too, as she looked at her time-telling machine and got up. We strolled back towards the entrance, passing a couple of people lying in the sun who recognised Sheila and hailed her, so she stopped for a chat. It turned out that they were the Essex couple, Val and Ken, who had been at the trivia quiz with her. I didn't know that Sheila had told them all about me and that, by a strange co... coi... coin... chance Val had read my previous diaries! "So this is the famous Truffles, then!" said Val, giving me a pat. "I've read your book, Truffles, and I loved it." I was rocked - unbelievable! Fancy us meeting someone, on a ship of all places, who had actually read my book. Val, you're my friend for life, I thought! I rubbed myself around her legs and then wished I hadn't because they were covered with that horrible oily stuff! Sheila laughed, "Well, Val, as I told you the other night, Truffles is going to be writing a new book about her experiences on the ship, so maybe you'll be in it now!" Everyone around laughed and looked at me – and, I don't mind telling you, I felt really chuffed! Ken and Val asked if she was planning to go to the trivia quiz that evening. "Yes," replied Sheila, "if it's before the show. If I bump into the Scottish couple anywhere I'll invite them to come, too, and we'll see if 'Team Triangles' can wipe the floor with the rest!" (What on earth is she talking about? I wondered. Surely they're not going to be doing the cleaning!) "It's earlier than the show, so we'll see you there then," the others said, and so we continued on our way.

We got into the elevator, which we had to ourselves, and rode down to Deck Five and the main shopping street. I wondered why we'd not gone straight back to the stateroom. By this time my tummy was making quite urgent noises and I didn't want my lunch to be held up for much longer. We walked up the street, and as we got to one of the drinking places Sheila stopped and spoke to a couple of people who were sitting outside it. These were her other trivia friends, Bobby and June. "I guessed you'd be here," said Sheila. "I know Bobby likes his tot of whisky before lunch!" June nodded, lifting her eyes to the sky, and Bobby raised his glass and said, "Och, this is yure wee cat then!" I could hardly understand what he was saying. He certainly didn't have a Cornish accent - it was an accent I had never heard before. And why was he calling me a 'wee' cat? It made it sound as if I had bladder problems! Mind you, I thought, I wouldn't mind a wee! All the more reason to get back to the balcony and my box. I pulled at the lead. "Okay, Truffles, I know you want your lunch," said Sheila. "I won't be a minute." The others chatted away for a while about this and that and I sat waiting impatiently. At last they finished their conversation and June said, "See you this evening at the quiz," and we made our way back. En route Sheila stopped at the general store and bought a packet of some crunchy things for herself. "I'm not going to have a big lunch today," she told me. "I'm going to sit outside with you and just have a coffee and crisps and some of the fruit." I wondered why. I know she likes to make the most of all the wonderful food she can get in the ship's special eating places, as she doesn't bother to cook much now she's on her own at home.

Back at the stateroom, I rushed out to the litter box while she was opening a letter she'd found. "Oh great," she said, "an official invitation to dine at the Captain's table on the last formal night. I was hoping I'd get one, but as I'm on my own now and not part of a couple I wasn't sure I would." I was puzzled. What was she going on about? She told me that for many years, whenever she and Peter had cruised with this particular company, they had been invited to dine with the Captain because they were on the VIP list (though she didn't tell me what VIP meant or exactly why they had got onto such a seemingly exclusive list). Oh well, whatever makes her happy, I thought. My lunch was much more important! I gave her a sharp miaow and she came down to earth again and filled my bowl with some shreds of salmon that she'd stored in the cold cupboard, topped with some of the cheesy treats she'd got in Gibraltar. Bang tasty, I thought!

We sat outside in the sun and I dozed whilst she idly flipped through her library book and some of the papers that were in the stateroom. I could get used to this sort of life!

Some time later Sheila went inside and I heard her opening and shutting doors and drawers, reappearing after a while wearing a smart new outer covering. I blinked. It was a bit early for her to change into evening attire. "I'm off to the Elegant Afternoon Tea Party," she said. Oooh, get you, I thought. How posh is that? Ah, now I realised why she didn't have much to eat at lunch - she was going to fill herself up with cakes! Cakes and chocolate have always been her downfall, that's why she's got the thighs she's always on about! "There won't be any canapé delivery today. I cancelled it because I knew I'd be out," she went on. She checked the time. "I'm a bit early," she said. "I don't want to be the first to arrive, so I'll hang on a bit." She sat down on the sofa and I dozed off again.

When I awoke she had gone. I stretched lazily and treated myself to a nice scratch. I do not have fleas, I might say; some drops that Sheila puts onto my neck keep the little blighters at bay, but there is nothing like having a good scratch. You know when you get an itch somewhere and you scratch it gently and then the more you scratch the more it seems to itch, and then the more you scratch the more pleasurable it gets? I'm sure you must know the feeling! I finally stopped scratching and went for a drink, and then I peered through the glass wall again at the C and the sky - nothing in sight except a flock of birds whirling overhead. Thankfully, they weren't Frigate Birds! I'm sure those black demons are going to haunt my dreams forever! This lot looked like the ordinary seagulls we see back home - nothing frightening about them. I sat and watched the white frothy stuff rushing behind us as we moved through the C and then went back to my corner. As I lay there, soaking in the sun, I was reminded of a cat joke that you might like to hear. I apologise to Val and other readers of my previous books, as I have included this joke in one of them before, but it might be new to the rest of you:

*Once upon a time there was a little cat who had died and gone to live in Heaven. After a few days God came to see how he was getting on. "I see from my records that you were a very good little cat when you lived on Earth," God said, "so is there anything that I can get you to make you feel at home here?" "Well," said the cat, "I've always wanted a lovely squashy beanbag bed, but my owners could never afford to get me one." "Of course you can have one," replied God. "I'll get it ordered." As God continued on his rounds, he met a group of little mice who had also recently died and moved into Heaven. "How are you all settling down?" God asked them. "Is there anything you'd like as a treat, as I know that on Earth you were all very good and well-behaved little mice?" "Oh, please, Mr God," said the mice, "we've always wanted to run faster, so we'd love some roller skates." God smiled and told them that he would get them some. About six months later, God was walking around and met the cat, who was lying in the sun on top of his lovely new squashy beanbag bed. "Hello, cat," he said. "How are you enjoying your new life up here?" The cat replied, "Oh, I'm having a great time! My bed is just so comfortable and the meals on wheels are delicious!"*

Time passed and Sheila returned. I greeted her with a purr and an ankle rub. "I enjoyed the tea," she said, "though I don't actually drink tea." Oh dear, I thought, here we go again - how can you drink T? It's a letter that is written down in your human words. You don't drink it, you write it! And, anyway, how come she enjoyed it if she didn't have it? My mind was boggling again! She continued, "Yes, well, I had my usual coffee, but oh, Truffles, the cakes and the little pastries and the sandwiches! It was just like being at The Ritz. There were also some handsome waiters to serve us - we all felt really special! Bit of a difference from my usual UN-elegant afternoon tea back home, with a mug of coffee and a bun!" she giggled to herself.

She took off her tea party outfit and put on the ship's towelling robe and paw covers. Then she spoke into the talking gadget by the bed before sitting on the sofa with a glass filled from the bubbly bottle. She started to watch the moving-picture machine. "I just ordered your dinner, Truffles," she remarked. "A real treat for you - pigeon tonight!" Pigeon, I gasped - bring it on! I've always craved the pair that I see sitting on the trees at the bottom of our garden, but I've never been able to reach one. Fancy them having pigeons on the ship! What next! This whole cruise experience was like a dream, and I was starting to think I never wanted to go home! But, there again, all good dreams come to an end. When I thought about it more sensibly, however, I didn't really think I wanted to spend the rest of my life surrounded by the dreaded C - our back garden was much more practical and I had all the little birds who lived in it to watch!

My pigeon dinner was duly delivered by Marcello. I was hopping up and down with anticipation. Their heady smell underneath the silver dome was driving me crazy! He remained chatting for a few moments with Sheila and, although he was a nice man, I was just willing him to go so that I could get cracking on the pigeons! As soon as the door had closed behind him, I pawed at Sheila's leg impatiently. "Goodness, Truffles!" she exclaimed. "Hold your horses!" (Why on earth is she suddenly bleating on about horses? I thought. I'm not interested in horses, I'm only interested in pigeons!) She extracted the pigeons and picked out the bones leaving me a nice bowlful of the meat, which she stirred into its delicious gravy. It tasted like pure nectar to me! "You polished that off in double-quick time," she said. "I can see I shall have to order you that dish again one night!" Too right, I agreed, licking my lips. When I carried out my after-dinner whisker-washing routine that evening I took my time - I wanted to keep the taste with me for as long as possible!

Meanwhile, Sheila had carried out her usual pre-evening ablutions and had changed into her third set of outer coverings that day. "I'm off now," she told me. "I've got to meet Connie and Ron at the Martini Bar for a drink, and then I'm going to the Trivia Quiz with the others. Hopefully it will finish before dinner - I wouldn't want to miss that after having no lunch." (Even with all those cakes inside you? I thought sarcastically!) "I'll see you later then, after the show," she said, stroking my head, before grabbing her handbag and leaving. I jumped up onto my cushion on the sofa and idly wondered what a Martini Bar was.

When Eduardo came in later on he seemed a bit flustered. "'Ello, Trufools," he said. "You 'av to wait for your teetbeet tonight. My boss come round soon and so I 'av to 'av everything look good quick!" You always make everything look good, I thought, so whatever it is, you don't have to worry about it! I retired to my bed in the corner and sat there quietly. I didn't want to get in his way, as he seemed so nervous. As usual, he worked quickly and ef... eff... effici... well, and he made a magnificent monkey (or maybe it was an ape?) out of a couple of the towels. He must be wanting to impress his boss, I reckoned. As he was just replacing the bubbly glass that Sheila had used, there was a knock at the door and two man crew members walked in, the first with a definite air of superiority about him. I can always recognise an air of superiority because, of course, I have one myself (except when being terrorised by giant black seabirds!) Eduardo stood to attention. The boss man smiled and told him to relax. "Eduardo, you are one of my best stewards," he said. "I've never failed you on an inspection yet!" He gave a cursory glance around the stateroom and bathroom. "Excellent, as usual," he said, nodding, and the man behind him wrote something down on the paper he was holding. "Ah," he said, noticing me in the corner, "this must be the cat we have on board. It's the first and only time we've ever allowed an animal on board. But I see no mess or cat hairs, so I am satisfied that you are handling things okay. Well done." I bristled a bit at what he was saying - I do *not* leave cat hairs about and I certainly *never* make any mess, and Sheila is most particular, as I am, about leaving my litter box in pristine condition all the time. But I guessed he had been sent here by the Elf and Safety people, so was only doing his duty. I had to keep reminding myself that I was, indeed, lucky to have been allowed on the ship in the first place. It was obviously an unheard-of thing! I heard Eduardo telling him that I had a litter box outside, which Sheila kept absolutely clean and that she disposed of my waste in the correct manner. He also told the boss how well behaved and quiet I was. I knew Eduardo was my friend! The boss and his sidekick departed and Eduardo breathed a sigh of relief. "Zey are very particular about hygiene on zis ship, Trufools, and zey 'av to be sure we do theengs proper!" I agreed with him. It was nice and reassuring to see that they double-checked every single thing - even though I didn't think I needed any more personal checking! "'Ere's teetbeet now, Trufools," he said, popping a plump sardine into my bowl. "Enjoy!" And I did ...

Much later Sheila came back. She seemed to be in a happy mood and a bit giggly. I supposed she'd had a few too many of those naughty drinks and frowned at her. "Oh, look! A monkey!" she said, picking up the towelling figure. "Isn't Eduardo clever?"

After a brief visit to her water box, she put on my lead and we went off for her usual casino session. We had to wait a while, as another person was sitting at Sheila's favourite machine. So she dragged me round the shops again, which were still open, and she nearly, I say nearly, bought another handbag. I heard her mutter to herself that, although she liked it, she'd hang on and see what was in the shops in port the following day when they were ashore, in case there was one she preferred. She had been keeping an eye on 'her' machine and saw that the person on it had given up in disgust when nothing had come out of it, so she claimed her place in front of it. "Now, Truffles," she said, "I might get lucky this time. Someone else has put a lot of money into it, so perhaps it's ripe for the taking!" No chance, dear, I thought! She stuck her little piece of paper into the machine's chest and started the button-pressing process again. Boring, boring, boring! I wondered if I could get away with not coming here the next night - I'd much rather just stay in bed sleeping! At least I was getting used to the noise in the casino by now and it just rippled over me like the squawking of a flock of seagulls! I was almost nodding off when a tremendous roar came from a crowd of people sitting round a nearby table, their eyes glued to a large, round spinning machine. The casino person sometimes threw a little ball into the rim of the big spinner and that was what the people were watching so closely. A man jumped up from his seat and everyone was patting him on the back and cheering. "Well," said Sheila, "he's had some good luck, but I don't think I'm going to get any tonight. Come on, let's go." And off for the usual Amoretto coffee session we went!

Whilst we were sitting there, the hossifer Sheila knew came up and joined us. "I hear you're going to be at the Captain's table on the last formal night," he said. "Perhaps I can sit with you at the dinner as you are all alone?" Perhaps her luck has changed for the better after all, I thought! "Yes, thanks very much, that'll be nice," she replied. Oh yes, I thought, she's playing it cool - that's a good move! He stayed a few more minutes talking and then left, saying that he'd see her with the Captain's other guests when they co... con... congr... met up for the pre-dinner drinks. With a brief salute, he smiled at her and walked away. Sheila looked down at me. "And don't you go reading anything into that, Truffles," she laughed, "he's much too young for me! But it will be nice to have an escort." She finished her drink and we returned to the stateroom.

When we got back Sheila picked up a card that was lying on the bed and read it. "Huh," I heard her mutter to herself, "madam won't like that!" She gave a wry grin. I didn't know what she was on about so I didn't take any particular notice. We carried out our normal bedtime routines and got into our respective beds. I switched on my sleep mode and was out like a light.

# The next day

We woke up early the next morning and once more bright sunlight had us both blinking. I went out and performed my morning ablutions, and then looked over the edge to see that we were parked up by the side of another dock, but this one was not nearly so big as the ones in Gibraltar or Southampton. There were a few buildings not far from us, but not all that big, and I could see green hills in the distance and leading up to them what looked like fields of strange, pale mauve-coloured grass. I could hear some lady humans singing out of tune, accompanied by some even more out-of-tune music. Looking down, I saw several people all dressed in odd-looking outer coverings and with funny hats on their heads. The ear-jarring music was coming from strange sets of pipes being played by three man humans. I must say that our local cats' chorus, which meets usually on a Saturday night on our neighbours' wall, sounds much better! Behind them were some outside shops selling lots of colourful things, but they were a bit far away so I couldn't see exactly what they were. Quite a large pr... pro... propor... part of what they were selling was in the same mauve shade as the grass in the fields. More useless stuff for Sheila to throw away her money on, I reckoned!

"Come in, Truffles," Sheila called, so I went back in. She nipped out and brought the litter box inside for some reason, and also the sack of catlit, and then she slid the doors shut behind her. I've usually eaten my breakfast outside, so I vaguely wondered why her routine had changed, However, I was more interested in my actual breakfast awaiting me in my bowl, which she'd placed on a sheet of paper near my bed in the corner of the stateroom. "I'm off for my breakfast now," she said, "as I'm getting off the ship early because I'm going shopping with Margaret in Provence." So that's where we are, I thought - not that it meant anything to me! It was just somewhere that wasn't in Cornwall! I finished off my meal and went to the patio doors, but they remained closed. I wanted to go out and sit in the sun as usual. Why had she shut me in? I felt a sulk coming on.

Just then Sheila returned. I went and sat by the doors, looking expectantly at her to open them for me. "I'm very sorry," she said, "but not this morning. You'll have to stay indoors, Truffles. Look, I've got to go now. Be good and I'll see you about lunchtime, or just after, I expect. You can go out later on this afternoon." With that, she gave me a pat, gathered up her ship's tote bag and her handbag and off she went.

I sat down, looking through the impenetrable (yes, another long word of yours that has somehow stuck in my brain over the years!) glass doors to the outside, and sulked. I had been dreaming of spending a nice morning lazing in the sun, but my dream had been shattered without any explanation.

As I sat there sulking, I thought I could hear a kind of roaring noise. It seemed to be coming from the stateroom on our left side, or rather from their balcony. It was definitely getting nearer and much louder. I stood up, my ears pricked. Suddenly all hell broke loose! From next door two members of the crew, dressed in matching white outer coverings and each holding what looked like a huge black snake in their paws, climbed onto our balcony and pointed the snakes' heads at the decking and the patio doors. Out of the snakes' mouths came a massive torrent of water! It made a horrific noise and I don't mind admitting that I was totally terrified! Like a bullet out of a gun, I shot up the curtains and jumped onto a narrow ledge that was above them, clinging on for dear life - my claws extended to full stretch! The noise of the water jets sounded like the torrential rain we get at home, which hammers horizontally on the windows, but what was happening outside here was much, much worse! I could hear another noise like the sound of a hundred mice pitter-pattering at full speed across a co... corr... corrug... tin roof. I realised it was the pounding of my heart! Everything on the ship so far had been lovely, but this experience was truly awful - a great deal more scary than even the nasty black bird! I prayed I would be safe up there - nothing was coming through the doors ... so far! I was shaking all over, but somehow I managed not to fall off the ledge. How long the torrents of water and the roaring sound went on I couldn't guess, but eventually the men moved over to the neighbours on our right and gradually the awful noise subsided as they got further away. The sound of the mice running over the tin roof faded into the distance. My goodness, this had been a real shock to the system and I should not be subjected to shocks like that at my age! How had Sheila let it happen? My tail wagged in anger. No wonder she was anxious to get out so early!

Help! Help! Scream! Scream!

I decided I would remain perched on the ledge indefinitely, as I felt comparatively safe there, in spite of the fact that my paws were beginning to feel numb from gripping on so tightly. The men and their snakes might come back again and this time I would be prepared! However, nothing happened, and after a while there was a knock at the door and Eduardo came in. He didn't see me at first. "Where are you, Trufools?" he said, looking all around.

Then he suddenly saw me and said, "Trufools, what *are* you doing up zere? Pleeze to come down, Trufools!" No way! I clung on defiantly, scowling at him with my tail wagging. Despite his pleas and some tempting shrimps that he waved in front of my nose, no way was I going to move. No way! At least not until Sheila came back, at which point I would be giving her a piece of my mind! He shrugged and said something in a language I didn't recognise, before starting on his morning chores. He continued busily changing the sheets and towels and doing all the other stuff he does, whilst calling up at me from time to time to come down. He was totally unsuccessful on that score! I was not moving until I was sure that nothing else was going to happen outside. Eventually, after calling to me one final time, he went.

Time passed; quite a lot of time. No more sounds came from outside and neither did Sheila return. It was the sight of the shrimps that Eduardo had left in my dish that finally persuaded me to surrender my perch! I jumped down. When I looked through to the balcony I could see that everything was soaking wet and there were pools of horrid water on the decking. There was certainly nothing I could do about what had happened, so I ate the shrimps and set about regaining my composure. Then I returned to my bed and carried on sulking.

Eventually I heard the card pinging in the door and Sheila

came in, carrying several bags. I sat up and turned my face to the wall. No way was I going to give her a welcome. "Oh dear," she said, "Have they been already?" She went over to the patio doors and looked out, noticing all the water. Then she came and picked me up and sat with me on the sofa, cuddling me. "Look, Truffles," she said, "when I read that card last night it told us that they were going to clean the balconies today, but I didn't know exactly what time. That's why I kept you in. I should have drawn the curtains, but you would only have gone under them and still looked out, so I didn't bother. I feared you might be frightened, but I couldn't just hang around waiting until whatever time they arrived. I'm really so sorry. You must have had a bit of a shock." A bit of a shock? I nearly had a heart attack! I was still livid, but she seemed genuinely apologetic so I had to forgive her, didn't I? She continued stroking me and soon I began to feel much calmer. She has that knack of comforting me if there's been some kind of drama. In a little while harmony between us was restored again!

Sheila tidied her shopping bags away and I saw that another neck ornament and another new handbag had appeared. "Well," she said, looking outside again, "there's no way we can go out yet, as it's still so wet. We'll have to wait until the sun has dried everything out. So, come on, we'll go up to the sun deck and have an ice cream, and then maybe we'll have a little game of golf so you can pat the ball about, as a treat after your terrible morning. And," she continued, "I'll order you the pigeon again this evening. How's that? Am I forgiven?" Okay, okay, yes she was! I wasn't sure what 'golf' was exactly, but the word 'ball' I did understand, so I knew it would be something nice!

We made our way up to the upper deck and Sheila found a chair. She left a towel on it and tied me to one of the legs, asking the people next door to keep an eye on me for a moment whilst she fetched an ice cream. They were nice people and were called Graham and Petra. They gave me lots of pats and I purred up at them. When Sheila and the ice cream returned, they all sat chatting and I heard her telling them how I came to be on the ship. Petra told Sheila that they cared for three cats called Moondoggie, Gidget and Chlöe and two dogs called Hampton and Parker. Crumbs, I thought, they had almost as many pets to care for as Sheila and Peter did when they had the house with the big garden. Besides me, they had four cats called Tansy, Lucky, Taro and Robbie and two dogs called Hennessy and Lady. Graham, Petra and Sheila continued reminiscing about past cruises while I half listened, vaguely noting that Petra had a strange accent, like Bobby and June did, but she didn't sound in the least like them. All I knew was that it was certainly different from the Cornish accent I was used to hearing. I think she came from some place "over the pond", as they described it, called something like Amerrika I think. Meanwhile, I licked up my share of the ice cream. It was so lovely and creamy and soft that I almost forgot the morning's trauma. Food is always a great healer!

Graham and Petra said that they were going to play golf too, so we all went a bit further along the deck and ended up where we'd seen all the little green areas where people were using long, thin sticks to try to get little white balls into little black holes. So this is golf, I thought. Well, I don't need a stick to get the ball in the hole - I'll paw it in and I bet I get mine in before Sheila does! Graham and Petra picked up two sticks and Sheila asked them if they'd mind if she borrowed one of them just to play the first two holes to see what I would do. They all laughed and looked at me. Well, don't just stand there, I thought, let me at it! Sheila took hold of a stick and tried to hit a ball into the hole. She was miles out! I smiled to myself. "Come on, Truffles, you have a go!" she said, letting my lead run out to its full length. Graham dropped a ball on the ground in front of me. Deftly, I swiped it right into the hole. They couldn't believe it! They all just looked at one another and appeared to be struck dumb! "That must have been a fluke," said Petra. No it wasn't, dear, I've had plenty of practice hooking mice in and out of holes during my long life! Sheila managed to get her ball into the hole after another three shots (!) and the others had their turn (they took two shots each, I noticed) and then we all moved on to the next patch of green. I noticed that this green stuff wasn't real like the big grassy area where Sheila had played the ball and hoop game with Connie and Ron. At the second 'green', Graham put the ball down for me and they all stood watching. By this time several other people were looking at me too. I'll show 'em, I thought! As before, I pushed the ball straight forward and into the hole with one swipe of my paw. There was stunned silence all round and then a burst of clapping! I smirked. "Goodness, Truffles," said Sheila, "I ought to put you on the stage! Come on now, we don't want everyone looking at us!" I love being the centre of attention but, even though I could have quite happily gone on demonstrating how to smack balls into holes for the rest of the afternoon, we left the others to continue their game and returned to sit down near to one of the water pools to enjoy some more sun.

Hole in one!

As the sun started to get lower in the sky we went back to the elevator meeting place. There were several people waiting and two were the ro... rot... rotu... well-covered Mr and Mrs Golightly. A man standing by us sighed. "Even if the elevator does turn up soon, none of us will be able to get in with *them* in there!" he said pointedly. The other people waiting all nodded in agreement. Mrs Golightly said nothing, but Mr Golightly turned round and shook his fat front paw menacingly at the man, who shrank back behind his wife! The élevator duly arrived and the Golightlys squeezed their way in ... just! The doors made several attempts to close. The unseen lady must have been getting a bit of a sore throat with continually having to say "doors closing". However, at last the doors did close, and the elevator groaned in sympathy and disappeared quickly downwards. "I bet it travels down faster than a scalded cat with them in it!" said the man whom Mr Golightly had threatened, looking down at me. Everyone nodded in agreement and tittered. "Just as well we couldn't get in it," said his wife. "I'd have been scared to death thinking we would drop right to the bottom of the shaft!" We did eventually get into another elevator before too long and hurried back to the stateroom - Sheila was looking forward to her canapés and I was looking forward to my pigeon dinner!

Back in the stateroom, Sheila looked out and saw the decking was more or less dry after the thorough dowsing it had been given earlier. She put the clean litter box outside again and I rushed straight on it for a solo performance, taking care to scuff plenty of granules over the sides! I was still a bit sore about what had happened earlier and so took great pleasure in watching her having to clean out the box again and brush up the spilt granules! She told me ruefully that I was a little monkey, and I knew exactly what she was thinking! All my life, if she or anything else has upset me, I have eased my temper by either giving something a good kicking (like a catnip ball or toy mouse) or else scuffing litter all around. It's a good feeling if you're a cat!

Anyway, peace now reigned and we sat outside until Sheila heard Marcello arrive with her treats. She greeted him and they chatted for a moment or two. Then she poured a glass of bubbly and brought out the bits and pieces and some of the fruit. "Oh, it's your lucky day," she said (well, I wasn't so sure about that!) taking off the lid and looking at the little tray. "There are some smoked salmon and jumbo prawn ones here, so you can have some of them - you wouldn't like any of the others. Only one prawn, though, I'm having the other!" We sat nibbling on our treats and then she went inside for the usual rummage around to decide what outfit she would wear in the evening and, what always seemed to take her far longer, which acc... acce... access... ornaments to wear with it. As I think I told you earlier, she will never wear the same thing twice on a cruise. I've always known that she has an awful lot of outer coverings (let alone the bags and paw covers!) but until I saw her on this trip I never realised quite how many she had! No wonder she's always complaining about all the washing and ironing! I've always said that there's just no need for all these outer coverings. We cats have a perfectly serviceable fur catsuit, which can be used for every occasion and only needs a quick lick-over once or twice a day to keep it in purrfect condition and looking good. On the other hand, I have to say that in my opinion when you humans do take off your outer coverings, well, you are such an unattractive pale pink colour underneath that no wonder you want to cover yourselves up!

Sheila watched the news and spoke into the machine by the bed to order my pigeons, which didn't take very long to arrive, and I savoured every mouthful. The food of the gods! I will never look at the two who live in our garden in the same way again! Unfortunately, I'm not as mobile as I was when I was younger, so nowadays I have no real chance of catching one. I have to be realistic about that. Great shame!

Off Sheila went to meet her friends for her own dinner, not forgetting her pre-dinner cocks' tails (or whatever they were called, I forget now) and probably some more naughty drinks after. Or maybe she would go to a trivia quiz, dancing or a show, or whatever. Still, I was pleased to see her enjoying herself, as I know she gets lonely sometimes just being at home, despite my sin... scin... scinti... terrific company. I settled down on my cushion to catch up on some sleep. With all the ups and downs of the day, I had by no means reached anywhere near the goal that I try to uphold of sleeping 22 out of every 24 hours!

When Eduardo arrived later he first peered round the door and he seemed relieved when he saw me comfortably sitting on the sofa. "Oh, Trufools, I so pleezed you okay," he said, coming over to pat me. "You worree Eduardo thees morning." I purred up at him. It was nice to be worried about. I felt a bit bad because I had been rude to him when I'd been up on the ledge, and he'd only been trying to be helpful. So I purred with added enthusiasm and rubbed my head on his hand. "Look 'ere," he said, "for you!" And he dropped two jumbo prawns in my bowl. Great! They didn't remain in the bowl for more than a few seconds, as they were immediately transferred to my tummy! I returned to the sofa, after allowing him to plump up my cushion, and stayed there while he hummed some sort of tune under his breath, working like a little beaver as usual. His towelling creation this evening was a giant creature that looked like a sort of fish, I thought, though I didn't recognise it. But then, my fish usually comes in tins!

After he'd finished and left I dozed on and off, still thinking about the morning's little drama and hoping that I wouldn't have nightmares about those big black snakes! Eventually Sheila turned up looking quite pleased with herself, so she must have had a good dinner, too. "Well, Truffles," she greeted me, "I've been to another great show and I met a nice couple called Suzy and Steve when I had my aperitif before dinner. They don't have a cat but have a lovely white dog called Boomer. He's as spoilt as you are! He even has his own white leather chair to match his fur! I'm going to have a drink with them tomorrow night, too." Oh dear, all these naughty drinks she's having, I tutted to myself. "Now," she went on, "are you coming to the casino? Maybe I'll get lucky tonight!" But no, I didn't want to go to that noisy casino again; I wanted to catch up on some sleep, so I turned around and curled up more tightly, hoping that she'd get the message! She did, so I was left in peace once more.

Much later she returned and let me out on the balcony, which was nice and dry again, thank goodness. Then we carried out our usual bedtime routines, and that was another day over - and one I certainly wouldn't forget in a hurry!

# Life on board

The next week passed by in something of a blur. Both Sheila and I had by now got right into the routine of the relaxing life on board a cruise ship. Indeed, I almost began to forget our home life back in Cornwall, I was so into this new, unheard-of for a cat, style of living! On several days Sheila went ashore at some exotic-sounding places: Livorno, Civitavecchia, Cagliari, Cádiz, Lisbon and Vigo. Strangely, each time she returned another handbag would appear on the shelf. I don't know what Eduardo must have thought! She appeared to meet up with her friend Margaret on her trips ashore, so the handbag shops in those towns must have done very well out of the two of them, with Sheila and Margaret no doubt matching each other bag for bag!

In the afternoons we usually spent some time after lunch on our own balcony, lazing in the sun - so Sheila could wear her shorts in private! Then she would change into some longs and we'd go up to the top deck, where I would lie on the grass and she would sometimes play a game with Connie and Ron or Graham and Petra. We never saw Mr and Mrs Golightly anywhere again! Then we'd have an ice cream. I wished we had a whippy ice cream-making machine back at home! Afterwards maybe we'd go down and stroll along the main shopping promenade and Sheila would give yet more of her money stuff away in return for sparkly things or treats or whatever. At this rate, I thought, she'll soon have no more money left! Sometimes, if there was a trivia session on somewhere, the 'Triangles' would take part, and one day Sheila came back to the stateroom very excited as they had won prizes! "Key rings!" she told me, putting hers into her pocket. What's a key ring? I wondered. Well, whatever it was, as I was unlikely ever to be the owner of a pocket, I guessed it wouldn't be of any use to me! On another occasion she dumped me back in the stateroom earlier than usual and rushed off to some lessons in how to salsa dance. She only ever went the once, which didn't surprise me - I mean, DO fairy elephants dance the salsa?! Sorry, readers, that really was a catty remark! I didn't mean it, Sheila! She did have some success, however, in another set of classes she attended. She made a teddy bear to add to her collection. It didn't quite match the standard of the one she had bought on the ship; it was a bit of a ama... amat... amate... cack-handed effort, but she was happy with it and called it Thread Bear!

She had met another couple on board: another Graham, but his lady was called Jacqueline. She told me that they ate with her on the table at dinner in the evening, along with Dianne and David. Well, not literally on the table, I mean they were actually sitting by the side of the table! I do find your ways of ex... exp... expre... making things clear still a bit difficult at times - sorry! I did meet them once when we were outside on the deck. Graham had been climbing the big rock - though he didn't shin up it anywhere near as quickly as I did! Jacqueline had been watching him and we happened to be passing, so we stopped to watch too. After what seemed an age, he got down to the bottom again, puffing a bit, and Jacqueline gave a sigh of relief. "I was worried you'd fall," she chided. "No, it was a piece of cake!" he said. Oh dear, here we go again, I thought. A piece of cake? It was nothing like any cake I'd ever seen - ah, perhaps it was a rock cake! I remembered Sheila once saying to someone that her old granny used to make lovely rock cakes, although I couldn't imagine how you would ever get a bit of a rock like that into your mouth! I decided I would stick to cat crunchy treats!

Talking of food, I had definitely got fatter since being on board on account of all my overeating - all those extra treats from Eduardo and all those lovely rich dinners! I found that, because my tummy seemed to have grown so, it was much more difficult for me to lick my nether regions! It was proving quite a strain on my back. I resolved that when I got home I would sadly have to cut down my food intake for a while. Still, the food at home wouldn't be so hard to resist, as tinned food isn't exactly inspiring. It's adequate and reasonably tasty, but it in no way compares to the gourmet standard to which I had now become ac... accu... accusto... used to on the ship!

On the evening before our last full day on board came Sheila's much-anticipated dinner on the Captain's table. It was also the final night, which meant that everybody would be wearing their best outer coverings and all the lady humans would be trying to outdo each other! In the daytime Sheila had got off the ship at a place called Vigo and when she returned she was carrying with her a very big bag. I wondered how on earth she was going to get all the extra stuff she'd bought home with us; it had been a big enough struggle carrying everything on here in the first place! Oh well, that was her problem, not mine!

After lunch she went off to the fur-dresser and I sat out in the sun as usual, but after a while I began to feel a bit of movement underneath me, which seemed to be coming from the ship. Up until now, ever since we left Southampton, you just couldn't have told it was even moving; it was only when you looked over the back and saw the trail of froth behind the ship that you realised we were going along pretty fast. I couldn't explain what the 'movement' happening now felt like. Everything had always been so very smooth and now, when I looked out from the balcony at where the edge of the C met up with the edge of the sky, it seemed to be moving slowly up and down. Most odd! As the afternoon went on, I could feel the floor sort of swaying. It felt rather like when you sit on a tree branch and the wind is blowing. Although somewhat strange, I rather liked the feeling - it was almost soothing and in a while it was kind of lulling me to sleep!

When Sheila came back from her visit to the fur-dresser, she came outside and I thought said we were in the bay of biscuits (or some name that sounded like that!) and it might be a bit rough for a few hours. I didn't have a clue what she was talking about, but she didn't seem particularly worried and said that this often happened in the bay of biscuits. As far as she was concerned, it made things a bit more interesting but many of the other passengers might not agree with her. As I said, I didn't know what she was going on about, so I just lay there and didn't take much notice.

She spent the rest of the afternoon trying on the new set of outer coverings that had come out of the big bag she had brought back from Vigo. Together with the fur-do she'd just had, she looked at her very best I must say. The top half of the outfit was mostly covered with thousands of tiny, round, shimmering silver, dark purple and light purple beads. She then spent ages matching the new outfit up with various of her sparkly bits and humming and hawing over what paw covers to wear and what handbag to carry. She was certainly 'going to town' (one of your human sayings!) for this evening's special dinner! When Marcello brought in the usual canapés, he looked at the shimmering outfit hanging up and said, "Oh, madame, you weel be belle of ball zees evening, eh?" "Well, I can but try!" laughed Sheila. What a lot of fuss you lady humans make when you go out somewhere special, I thought. An extra five-minute body lick is all we cats need to do for an important date!

After she had got everything sorted to her satisfaction, Sheila made herself a cup of the frothy stuff and we sat together on the sofa, as outside the sun had disappeared and it did seem a bit unsteady on the balcony. "I thought it was going to be a bit rough," she remarked. "It had to be tonight of all nights, didn't it?!" Still, the rocking didn't stop us from eating our afternoon treats - some venison pâté on teeny-weeny bits of crispy bread for me and I don't know what else for her! Then I dozed for a while and she watched the moving pictures on the wall, glass of bubbly in hand!

The swaying movement of the ship seemed to be getting worse. I noticed that my bed had slid from its corner right across to the opposite corner of the room! Mind you, nothing else seemed to have moved - nothing had fallen off the shelves or off the table, though I did notice that Sheila had been careful to keep tight hold of her glass of bubbly! She got up and went over to the talking machine to order my dinner, and I could that see she was lurching about a bit. Surely just one glass of the bubbly stuff couldn't have made her squiffy already, I thought! Then I got up and I, too, felt a bit unsteady on my paws - only for a second or two, though, soon regaining my balance. As you probably know, cats can cling on to anything, be it moving or still. I wondered why the bay of biscuits was doing that to us.

Sheila swayed over to the bathroom and I heard a crash and one of those words you humans shouldn't say in public as she dropped something on the floor. I got back onto the sofa and sat firmly down on my cushion whilst she finished her ablutions, and then she spent a further half-hour in front of the looking glass fiddling with her face and her claws, which she was painting a very pale purple colour - her claws, I mean, not her face!

Very soon my dinner arrived - lobster! Great! I waited impatiently whilst she chopped it up and decanted it into my bowl. "Better put on some lower heels, I think. It's still rough, and I don't want to fall over in front of the Captain," she muttered. "Bye, Truffles." Then, with one final glance at herself, off she went for her big evening. I continued with the lobster. Very nice! Afterwards I got back on the cushion, cleaned up my whiskers and settled down again. The regular rocking and swaying movement soon lulled me to sleep. But suddenly I had a rude awakening! After what must have been a much stronger lurch of the ship, my cushion and I suddenly landed on the floor! By now the floor was definitely swaying more violently and I began to feel rather na... nau... naus... sick. I am hardly ever sick and can't remember being so since I was a kitten, except perhaps occasionally when I've gulped down my food too fast. Oh yes, and once I had a very nasty moment after I'd eaten a frog! Well, I didn't want to embarrass myself by throwing up here, so I made my way over for a drink of water, which was slopping about a bit in the bowl, and had a few laps. Good, I felt instantly better!

Sheila hadn't warned me that ships sometimes rocked like this! It wasn't frightening or particularly unpleasant, just a rather strange feeling. I sat on the floor and leant against the sofa whilst the rocking continued to get even worse, causing some of the coloured fruits to roll out of their bowl onto the floor and the papers to slide off the table. Fortunately, Sheila's bottle of bubbly remained solidly wedged in its container. I heard one or two things toppling over in the bathroom, but I didn't go to investigate. Well, Eduardo would be here soon and he would see that everything was okay. I remained where I was ...

By the time he arrived, I felt that the rocking was not quite so violent. "'Ello, Trufools," he greeted me, "are you okay?" He bent down and stroked me and replaced the cushion on the sofa. I got back into it. "Lots times eet iz bit ruff 'ere in zee bay," he said, "but getting beeter now. Look, I got you soom cheecken. You eat, eh?" Oh yes, I definitely ate it! Then he put things back into their right places, changed the towels and stuff and finally turned the bed down, laying his latest towel masterpiece down on top of it. I wasn't sure exactly what it was supposed to be, though! Tonight I noticed that he put extra choccies out for Sheila. That'll please her, I thought. A final pat for me and then he was gone.

Much later Sheila returned, holding a single red flower and also a large picture. I know you humans like to make pictures of each other. I have had lots of pictures made of me, too. The stateroom was still swaying slightly. I had wondered if she would also be swaying of her own accord if she'd had too many of the naughty cocks' tails, but she seemed no different from normal. I guessed the dinner had gone well. "I had a lovely time, Truffles," she said, sitting on the sofa beside me. "The officer I know sat next to me and the Captain was opposite, and the other people on the table were all charming. They took a photo of us all. Look!" She showed me the picture, but, although she was obviously pleased with it, I can't really see pictures like you do, so it didn't make much impression. "The food we had was superb," she went on, "and the Captain spoke to everyone and was telling jokes. One was about how when you are in a big ship all small ones have to get out of the way. So I told him the true story of old Jim the fisherman and he really laughed!" I had heard this story many times before, but I think you might like to hear it too! This is how Sheila tells it:

*A lot of naval ships are based in Devonport, Plymouth, and where the river joins the sea is called Plymouth Sound.*

*There is a special area out there where the frigates and other large naval vessels used to carry out a procedure called 'swinging the compass'. I don't know if it's still done nowadays, but it's all a bit technical for me anyway! However, on one occasion old Jim (when he was younger!) was out with his father in their little fishing boat and a large navy frigate was looming down on them. Its Captain shouted out through a megaphone: "Get out of the way!" However, the fishing boat carried on regardless! The frigate got nearer. The Captain leant out of the bridge window and shouted again: "I order you to turn aside! I am the Commander of this ship!" And Jim's father stood up and bellowed back: "And I'm the skipper and owner of this one!" (But they did move out of the way!)*

"Right, Truffles," said Sheila, "let's go to the casino! I feel in a winning mood! It's my last chance, as tomorrow night we'll be in bed early as we'll be getting off first thing on Saturday. So come on, we'll go now and then I can have my last lovely Amoretto coffee! It'll be back to normal again when we get home - instant out of a sachet!" I let her dress me in my 'formal night' diamanté collar and we set off. By now it seemed to me that the ship was hardly rolling at all, though there were still some passengers tottering past us who looked a bit pale. Sheila had told me earlier that she had never felt seasick (as she called it), so I didn't let on that I'd had an anxious moment back in the stateroom! She had said that some people would always feel ill at the slightest rocking of a ship, so she couldn't understand why on earth they would choose to go cruising! On the other hand, others, like herself, would have no problems even in the strongest winds.

The casino was even more th... thr... thro... crowded and noisy than normal. Everyone else must have been feeling in a winning mood too! People were standing several deep around the tables and nearly every machine had some person frantically pressing its buttons! By a stroke of luck (excuse the pun!) Sheila's favourite machine was sitting there all alone. She sat down and I assumed my usual position underneath her seat, from where I could observe the comings and goings of the crowd without getting trodden on. "Well, Truffles," she said, "I've not really lost too much this trip. But, there again, I've not won much either! I always expect to lose my initial stakes anyway." Steaks? She does drift off so, I thought. One minute she's talking about winning money and then she's on about meat! Oh well ... "But all told," she continued, "it's taken quite a lot of my money over the past fortnight, so now it's payback time! I'm going to double my stake tonight - you've got to speculate to accumulate - as it's my last chance, so let's hope!" Some hope, I thought gloomily - she'll just be throwing her money away!

I heard her above me continually pressing the buttons and sometimes the machine was making the loud jangly sound she loves to hear when it pays out. At other times I would hear her mutter a naughty word under her breath! But after quite a while and much effort, things finally paid off for her - I couldn't believe it! The machine was making a horrendous noise that seemed to go on and on and things inside its tummy were whirring, clinking and pinging! The people next door were laughing - not so much as Sheila, though! "Blimey," she screeched, "it's not the jackpot, but very nearly! That's given me back all I've put in and more besides!" She pulled out the bit of paper from the machine's chest and dragged me over to the corner of the room where two lady casino people were sitting behind a counter. Sheila passed over her bit of paper. "You've done well - $375!" said the person, smiling at her, and she put several pieces of paper money into Sheila's paw. "Thanks," replied Sheila. "See you again next May!" And she dragged me off again.

"Is she winning at last?"

Up to the next deck we went and, sitting down at her usual table in the coffee place, she ordered her Amoretto drink and, what's more, a large piece of Amoretto cake! "Might as well indulge," she muttered. "Back to normality soon and a strict diet!" Me too, I thought ruefully! I was feeling very portly and didn't want the cats next door to be laughing behind my back if they saw me waddling around the garden! We sat companionably together and a few people that Sheila knew passed by and stopped for a chat. They were all disappointed that the cruise was nearly over, and I realised that I was sorry that my 'once in a lifetime' experience was about to finish, too. I say 'once in a lifetime', but perhaps I should rephrase that - it should be 'once in a nine lives time'! Cats have nine lives, as you probably know - though after the vile bird and water-spewing snakes episodes, my personal life level has now dropped to seven!

Sheila looked at the little time-telling machine strapped to her paw (sparkling with diamanté like my collar, I noted) and seemed amazed that it had got so late. "Goodness, Truffles," she said, "it'll be nearly time for breakfast soon. We must go!" And so we went!

Back at the stateroom and bereft of our finery, we sat and looked at each other. She patted me. "Well, that's about it, Truffles. Home soon and back to normality! When it gets to the end of a cruise I always feel I've just got into the swing of things and into the shipboard routine, and wish I could stay on for another week!" I nodded in agreement. But, nice as it had been, I was eager to get home and out into the garden to check on the local bird populace! I also intended to brag about my exploits to the cats next door!

It had been a late night, so our beds looked inviting. After I had thankfully used the litter box and she had eaten the bedtime choccies, we called it a day and sleep came very quickly to both of us!

# Our last full day on board the ship

We awoke quite late the next morning and Sheila quickly went through her morning ablutions, cleaned out the trusty litter box, brushed me and gave me my breakfast of tinned turkey morsels and crunchies. I'll have to get used to living out of tins again all the time now, I thought sadly. Then she went off to enjoy her own last mega cooked breakfast before it was back home to the usual unappetising dry bits of straw that she normally has. I was sitting gazing out at the C when Eduardo arrived. "It's ze last time I see you in ze morning, Trufools," he said. "You good cat - 'ere's last breekfest treat," and he put a large and very plump sardine into my bowl. I purred at him in thanks and rubbed around his legs. He really had been such a nice man and had been very kind to me. I liked him. I polished off the sardine whilst he busied himself about the stateroom as usual. When he left I wondered who would be living in our stateroom for the next trip. I bet there wouldn't be another cat! What would Eduardo do with all his excess prawns and sardines now? I mewsed. I supposed he'd have to eat them all himself!

Sheila wasn't too long and she told me to stay on the balcony out of the way while she did our packing. I was quite happy; it was still sunny, though not nearly so warm as it had been in the foreign places we'd visited. Well, I certainly hoped that the packing wouldn't take half so long as it did before we came on the cruise, or she'd never get it finished before we got to Southampton - especially with all the extra handbags she'd bought, not forgetting the teddy bears! I forgot to tell you that she had bought another teddy from somewhere ashore, who wore a straw hat with 'Roma' on it! I dozed in my sunny corner, but after a while it got windy so I went inside.

Finally Sheila snapped the last of the large cases shut and at... att... attac... fixed on the labels. "Still lots to carry," she groaned. "Oh well, I suppose it's my own fault for buying so much! Still," she brightened, "at least all that money I won in the casino will help pay off my credit card!" She dragged the cases over to one side of the stateroom and told me she was off for a late lunch. Dropping some crunchies into my bowl, she left. To be honest, I didn't feel very hungry at all, so for probably the first time on record I didn't eat them!

I continued to sit outside, and now I could see that in the far distance there was land in sight. There were also a lot of other ships around us - all shapes and sizes; mainly like the grubby ones I had seen in the docks all loaded up with whatever ships get loaded up with. I only saw two others like ours - people carriers - but I was pleased to see that we were still the biggest!

Sheila returned and clipped on my lead, saying that we were going for a last stroll around, though not outside because it was very windy, and at the same time she could return her library book. We trekked over to the elevator. The unseen voice told us the doors were closing and then announced that we had arrived at the deck where the library was. I gave up wondering where the unseen lady was hiding - I guess it was just one of those mysteries I would never solve! When we arrived at the library I was amazed again at seeing so many books all in one place - shame mine weren't among them! Sheila added hers to the shelf, saying that she'd not finished it; she never did on a ship, as there were too many distractions! So why did she bother getting it in the first place then? I thought uncharitably. I pulled on the lead - I was fed up with this library place already! "Okay, okay," she said, and we left and went down several sets of stairs until we arrived at the shopping road.

As we strolled along we suddenly came across Margaret, who was laden down with bags once more. Did she live in shops? I wondered. She and Sheila could shop for England, that's for sure. They found some seats and sat down and I lay beside them and people-watched. It seemed very busy and there was a large crowd forming by a table, with crew people wearing matching white coats and hats standing behind it. They seemed to be cutting and chipping away at big blocks of stuff that looked like glass. Well, that wasn't a surprise on this ship, I thought - everywhere you went there was glass! But I soon realised that it wasn't glass, because as they cut away at it I could see what looked like drops of water coming out of it and collecting in little puddles at the base of the blocks. Then it hit me - the shapes they were making were something like Eduardo's towelling animals! Eventually they finished and the crowd clapped their paws together excitedly. Standing on the table were a big dolphin, a horse's head, a lion and an elephant. Very clever! Sheila and Margaret took out their little picture-making machines and took pictures of the animals. Then Sheila said goodbye to Margaret and told her she would keep in touch. Margaret patted me and we parted. She went back into the shop selling sparkly neck decorations and we continued on to the far end of the road. "That's as far as we go, Truffles," said Sheila, and so we made our way back again, past the shops and past the drinking places. When we reached the car with the giant teddy bears sitting in it, she stopped, lifted me up and placed me in between them, and then took our picture! Finally we arrived at the general store, where she bought some choccy bars (naughty, naughty!) and a pack of biscuits. Then it was back to the stateroom.

As it was still windy, Sheila slid open the patio doors, just leaving a gap big enough for me to squeeze through to get to my box. She then went out again, saying that she was going to the internet café to send some messages. She had never mentioned this internet café place before. I know that in cafés people drink the brown frothy stuff she likes, but I wondered what a cup of internet looked and tasted like. I slipped outside, but not for long - I hate wind!

The rest of the afternoon passed by and eventually Sheila returned, only a few moments before Marcello arrived with her last plate of canapés. She would miss those, I thought! She ate the lot herself this time, without offering me any! I suppose it was my own fault, because she'd seen that I hadn't eaten the crunchies! She sat down on the sofa and drank the remainder of the bubbly whilst watching the moving pictures on the wall. I came and hopped up beside her. "Oh well, Truffles," she said, "we must make the most of our last few hours on board. All good things have to come to an end. I've had a great time and I hope you have, too!" She raised her glass. We sat.

The time came to order my dinner, so she turned to me and asked if I'd like the pigeon again one last time. Too true I would! And when it arrived I savoured every mouthful, as I knew I'd never eat the likes of it again unless by some million-to-one chance I managed to catch one of the errant pigeons that lived at the bottom of our garden. And, even so, they wouldn't be cooked in such a tasty sauce as these! Sheila got washed and changed and went off for her last dinner, too. I wondered what she would choose. As I never went with her to eat, I really have no idea what she scoffed throughout the cruise. All I know is that, whatever it was, it must have filled her up, as she was now looking a bit on the fat side - although thankfully not in the same class as that Mrs Golightly!

Eduardo came in later as usual and he was carrying one of those little picture-making machines in his paw. "'Ello, Trufools," he said, "I take picture to remember you." That's nice, I thought, and I sat up on the sofa, giving him my best pose - head up, ears pricked and tail curled neatly around me. I gave him my best Cheshire cat grin and he grinned back at me. "Zank you, Trufools," he said. "You good cat!" He gave me a pat and produced a lovely chunk of steak. I fell on it eagerly. I would miss all these gourmet treats! Now I knew why Sheila liked the ship food so much, if it was to the same standard as I had been getting! She would feel as let down as I would be going back to tinned food when we got home, though in her case it would be back to a diet of slimming soups and straw biscuits! I sat and watched Eduardo for the last time as he went about his chores, humming under his breath. I noticed that he'd left two choccies on Sheila's bed tonight but no towel animal. With one last pat from him and an ankle rub from me, we said our farewells and he went out, leaving me feeling a little sad. I had enjoyed his company over the past two weeks.

Sheila returned much earlier than usual and she, too, was looking less than happy. She sat by me on the sofa and we looked sad together!

Then she stood up and took off her evening outer coverings, slipping them inside one of the suitcases and covering herself with the ship's robe. With great effort she hauled the three cases to the stateroom door and shoved them through it. "That's it," she remarked. "All ready to go now!" She made herself a large cup of frothy coffee. I bet she's sorry she hasn't got any Amoretto to put in it, I thought. We sat on the sofa side by side and she set the moving-picture machine going. She watched; I dozed.

Not too long afterwards we went to our respective beds. I lay awake for some time, going over all that had happened. I could now quite clearly see why so many of you like this cruising way of life. All the pa... pam... pamp... being looked after so well; and the best thing of all, the terrific food! I admit that I am looked after very well at home, and until I ate on the ship I had been quite satisfied with my food. I sighed. The steak, pigeons, lobster, etc., could only remain in my memory now, and I resigned myself to eating tinned food again! At least Sheila doesn't give me 'own brand' tins any more. I had rebelled against them once and she cap... capi... capitu... gave in and has never bought them since! I turned over and went to sleep.

# Leaving the ship and going home

We woke up to see grey skies. The sun had not bothered to come out and greet us at Southampton. Much earlier than usual, Sheila made me go outside and told me to hurry up with my toilet routine. I wasn't sure what was going to happen this morning, so instead of taking my time and enjoying the procedure I thought I'd better do as I was told for once! Anyway, it wasn't very inviting out on the balcony now. I looked out at the large grey buildings opposite and I could see right below us on the dockside lots and lots and lots of suitcases. I blinked. There were more suitcases heaped down there than there were books in the library! Dock people, looking not much bigger than ants from our lofty position, were sc... scu... scur... rushing about and lifting them onto strange-looking motor machines, which then took them out of sight into one of the grey buildings. "Come in, Truffles," Sheila called. "I want to get on. Come and get your breakfast!" I went inside and ate the food she'd put into my bowl with little glee. Meanwhile, she emptied the litter box and rinsed it out and then packed the rest of my stuff away in my holdall. At least the catlit sack was finished now, so that was one less thing for her to carry - though looking at the pile of extra bags waiting on the sofa, I wondered how on earth she was gong to cope with it all. Still, not my worry! My bed and cushion now packed away, I curled up on the carpet and awaited events.

She made herself a coffee and ate some of the biscuits that she'd bought the day before. I wondered why she hadn't gone out for her usual breakfast. Perhaps it was too early? She then went all round the stateroom and the bathroom opening every door and drawer and even checking under the bed. What was she looking for? Anyway, whatever it was, she didn't find it. Then she sat down, not looking too concerned, so it didn't seem as if she'd lost anything. She finished the remainder of the biscuits and then went into the bathroom, and I jumped as I heard the sudden roar of the flush again. Well, I certainly wouldn't miss that horrendous noise, I reflected. She came out. "Just one more check around to make quite sure I haven't left anything," she muttered, and then once again she repeated what she'd done not ten minutes earlier! She walked all around the stateroom, opening and closing the doors and drawers yet again! What a waste of time, I thought. We cats would only ever have to do a check once; we weren't so stupid that we would so soon forget what we had just done! It must be her age, I decided.

Sheila clipped my lead on my collar and put on her top outer covering, which had been lying on the bed. "How I'm going to carry all this lot I really don't know," she said. I wondered, too! Anyway, somehow she attached a couple of carrying bags to the long handle of her wheel-along suitcase and balanced her ship's tote bag on top of it, which was now bulging - with the mysterious totes, I supposed. Then she slung two more, smaller bags over her shoulder and picked up her handbag and my lead. We staggered towards the door, only to be faced with the problem of getting it open with just her one free paw! After all that loading up, she then had to put everything down on the floor again, tutting as she did so! She then opened the door and leant the case against it, allowing us to wriggle through before slamming it shut. She then set about balancing everything again. People walked by, offering looks of sympathy. All they seemed to be carrying were just one or two small bags each, not the entire contents of a shop!

We made our way slowly but surely to the elevator meeting point, where many other people were waiting. Looking at all the bags they were holding, which were taking up a lot of extra space, I reckoned we were going to have a long wait to get inside one! In fact, I decided that we'd probably need nearly a whole one to ourselves! Eventually we got lucky when two arrived together. We managed to get in one containing only one man with a small sack over his shoulder. He took pity on Sheila and offered to carry some of her stuff to the gangway, and she was relieved to take up his offer! She told him that we were not getting off just yet, but were going to wait in a special room that was reserved for certain passengers - ah yes, I drew myself up proudly, special, important passengers like us! My snobby side was coming out again, readers! Anyway, the kindly man accompanied us to the special room and then bade us farewell, wishing us a good journey home. Sheila thanked him effu... effus... effusi... very much.

When we entered the special room I saw around another ten people sitting there with their luggage in comfy chairs and drinking frothy coffee or those - sickly sweet but not necessarily naughty - fruity drinks. A pretty young lady crew member greeted Sheila and asked if we'd enjoyed the trip, and Sheila told her, of course, that we had! "So this is Truffles," smiled the lady, stroking my head. "I hope she's going to say some nice things about us!" "I'm sure she will," replied Sheila. "Are you being met at any particular time?" asked the lady. "You can get off at any time you want, you know, you don't have to wait until they call your luggage group." "Yes, I know," responded Sheila. "We'll just wait here until 8.30 and then we'll go. A taxi is coming to take us back to Cornwall." "Fine," said the lady. "Let me know if there's anything you want." Then she went off to greet another two passengers who had just come in - carrying their one small bag each!

Sheila, the heap of luggage and I sat down for a while and she drank some of the horrid sickly fruit juice. Ugh, it turned my tummy just to smell it! Then she got out her little talking machine and I heard her speaking into it to Tony. "Come on, Truffles," she said, "he's nearly here, so we'll get off now."

We got up and she loaded up again. The kindly lady crew member opened the door for us and said she hoped she'd see Sheila again on her next trip. We started to make our way slowly along the passageway and then suddenly, of all people, Sheila's friendly hossifer appeared. "Oh, let me carry some of that for you!" he smiled. "You're a godsend," she replied, offloading most of the bags onto him! We all made our way, at a much quicker pace than before, towards the hole in the side of the ship where everyone was leaving. Sheila and the hossifer were chatting away and I heard him saying that he would look forward to seeing her when she came on board next May. I bet he says that to all the lady humans, I thought to myself! When we got to the entrance Sheila put our stateroom cards into the machine that pinged and we stepped out onto the long, sloping, zig-zag pathway that led down into the dockside building. Sheila's hossifer went with us all the way to the entrance of the building, wished us a safe journey home, patted me and then went back onto the ship again.

We carried on until we reached an enormous space, where there were hundreds and hundreds of people looking amongst thousands and thousands of suitcases, trying to spot theirs! The noise was horrific. I shrank back nearer Sheila. It sounded as if yet another not very pleasant new experience was awaiting me. Sheila bent down. "It's okay, Truffles," she whispered in my ear, "we shouldn't be too long in here. I just have to find a porter with a trolley and get our luggage. I promise I won't let you go - don't be scared." Well, I wasn't scared exactly, just taken aback once more by the sheer number of people, the noise they made when all talking at once (or shouting more like) and their many, many suitcases. I think what has struck me the most about my cruising adventure is that everything, just everything on the whole trip, had just been so BIG! From the mountain with windows that was the ship itself to the mountain that was Mrs Golightly, and everything in between!

Sheila spotted a line of porters leaning against narrow platform things, which I presumed were their trolleys, and one of them came over. He was a cheery-looking man with lots of pale yellow fur on his head. "Blimey, madam," he said, scratching the aforesaid fur, "is that a blooming cat? Did you get it in Catalonia - or maybe the Cat and Canary Islands?" He laughed at his own joke. Sheila laughed, too. "No," she told him, "this is Truffles, my own very special cat, who has been on a very special journey!" He looked blankly at her and she briefly filled him in. Then he piled all our bags onto his trolley. "Does the cat want to sit on top?" he asked. "No thanks," replied Sheila, "I don't think she'd be very keen!" No, I jolly well wasn't. After travelling in style in motor machines and giant luxury ships, no way was I going to travel on some rusty, rickety old trolley! Sheila started wending her way up and down some of the lines of suitcases and very quickly found two of hers, which the porter loaded onto the trolley, but there was still one case missing - the one carrying all her paw covers and handbags apparently. Heaven help us all if she didn't find that one, I thought! After a few more trips up and down the lines of cases, Sheila eventually spotted the errant case and the man got it onto the trolley, which was now groaning with all the weight. There were whole families passing by with less stuff on their trolleys than Sheila had on hers!

We followed the porter towards the far end of the building, where I could see that there were two ways out, one with a red sign over it and one with a green one. We were headed in the direction of the green one. There were several fierce-looking people standing there, dressed in the same drab outer coverings as the unpleasant man at the dock entrance when we had first arrived at Southampton. These people were waiting right by the entrance, staring - rather rudely, I thought - at everyone going past. As we were walking through, one waved his paw at Sheila and said, "Just a minute, madam, if you please." I heard Sheila catch her breath. What now? I thought. Our porter halted the trolley, but the fierce man didn't seem to be very interested in that. Instead, he looked down at me. "What's that?" Oh no, not again, I thought. What IS it with these people? Haven't any of them seen a cat before? I glared up at him. "You can't bring an animal like that in here," he continued. An animal like *that*? How dare he! I am not, repeat not, a *that*! I am a famous *cat*! My tail began to wag. It was Sheila's turn to respond and she did indeed, showing him all my papers and the original invitation. "Well," he puffed, "it's all very irregular indeed. I've never come across such a thing before." "There's always a first time," said Sheila, smiling sweetly. Don't an... ant... antag... get him all worked up, I thought. He looks pretty nasty to me. The man pondered for a bit. Other passengers were going on through, looking at us. I was not pleased. I like to be looked at and admired, of course I do, but I do not like to be looked at for all the wrong reasons! The man gestured for us to go forward, but he told Sheila that he wanted to examine my collar. "What on earth for?" she asked. "You might have some drugs hidden inside it," he sniffed. "Well, be my guest," she said, "but don't you dare let Truffles go or you'll be in great trouble, I am telling you!" She gave him a glare that was as good as his! "Put the cat on the table," he growled at her. I was growling too, under my breath, and my tail was whipping from side to side. Sheila lifted me up onto the table and held me tightly whilst he undid my collar. I seized my opportunity and gave him a scratch, and I was gratified to see that I had drawn blood! He said one of those words that humans shouldn't use! I resolved never to wear that collar again once we were home, not after his horrible paws had been all over it. Ugh! He looked very closely at the collar and felt it all over inside and out - he even tried the stitching - and, of course, found nothing. "Okay, you can put it back on the cat now, madam, and carry on," he said. Then he turned and walked off without a backward glance. Sheila, the porter and I looked at each other in disbelief for a moment, and then we too walked off!

Outside we saw Tony coming towards us with a big, welcoming smile - somewhat different from the nasty man inside! "I wondered where you'd got to," he said. "We met a rather prickly customs man," replied Sheila. "I'll tell you about it later!" We walked towards the spot where Tony had parked his motor machine and the porter dumped the luggage on the ground beside it. Sheila thanked him and pressed something into his paw, and he gave me a pat on the head and walked off, making that odd whistling sound that you humans make when you're happy.

Sheila settled herself into the motor machine, with me curled up comfortably on her lap, and we set off on the long road back to Cornwall. By this time I was feeling quite tired and so I never took much notice of what was going on outside the motor machine as we sped along, getting nearer to home every minute. I dozed. Halfway there we stopped at the place where Sheila and Tony had had the toasted tea and cakes before, and they had some more. I walked about to stretch my legs. This was probably the last time I would have to experience being on a lead. That was a nice thought. I didn't think I could've stood being put on a lead every single day like a dog! Cats are just so much more independent than dogs; we don't need leads or to be guided to where humans want us to go, we go where *we* want to go! And, what's more, leadless!

Eventually we arrived back in familiar territory and Sheila woke me up as we entered our village. Tony stopped the motor machine in the driveway and we got out, both of them stretching their cramped legs after the long journey. I felt fine, as I'm used to sleeping curled up in one position for long periods! In fact, that, plus eating well, is my sole aim in life nowadays!

Sheila opened the front door and Tony heaved all the suitcases and bags into the hallway. "We seem to have twice as much as when we started," he laughed. Sheila thanked him profusely and he patted me and said, "Oh, well, next time I see you, Truffles, I'll have brought your mum all the way back from Southampton again, but I'll only have to collect you from the cattery just ten minutes away!" Yes, well, don't remind me, I thought, giving him a farewell purr! He drove away with a cheery wave and Sheila miserably surveyed the mound of luggage she would now have to haul up the stairs. I expect she was also thinking of how she would be paying for all her enjoyment by spending the next week doing nothing but washing and ironing!

Whilst she checked that everything was okay in the house, I popped out into the back garden to check (a) that it was still there, and (b) that the birds were, too. They were, and singing their hearts out - to welcome me back! Everything was back to normal. My experience on board a cruise ship, however, had been anything but normal, and I now know why it is that you humans find cruising so addictive! All the F's - Fabulous food, a Fantasy lifestyle and, most importantly, Fun!

Happy cruising, everyone!

*__Truffles__*
X

www.apexpublishing.co.uk